PRINCIPLES AND PRAGMATISM

KEY DOCUMENTS FROM
THE AMERICAN TASK FORCE ON PALESTINE

Edited by
Hussein Ibish & Saliba Sarsar

American Task Force on Palestine
Washington, D.C.
October 2006

Copyright ©2006 by the American Task Force on Palestine

ISBN 0-9785614-0-6

Published by the American Task Force on Palestine
815 Connecticut Avenue
Suite 200
Washington, D.C. 20006

Tel. (202) 887 0117
www.americantaskforce.org

All rights reserved. No part of this publication may be reproduced, stored in a retrieval system, or transmitted, in any form or by any means, electronic, mechanical, photocopying, recording, or otherwise, without the prior permission of the American Task Force on Palestine.

CONTENTS

Introduction..1

1. ATFP Mission Statement...5

2. Six Principles Towards a Fair and Lasting Solution
   to the Israeli-Palestinian Conflict................................7

3. ATFP Statement of Principles on Jerusalem................9

4. ATFP Statement of Principles on the Palestinian Refugee Issue.....11

5. A Vision for the State of Palestine:
   The Nature and Character of the State.......................13

6. Strategies for Advocating Palestinian Statehood........21

7. On Consensus and Alliance.......................................27

8. The Transformation of Palestinian Political Culture........31

9. The Future of Jerusalem..35

10. Palestine and Israel: Unkind History, Uncertain Future.....45

11. On the Historic Compromise...................................53

12. The Way Forward in the Middle East......................63

Postscript..77

ATFP's Executive Staff and Board of Directors...........79

The Editors...81

i

INTRODUCTION

The American Task Force on Palestine (ATFP) was founded in 2003 in order to provide an independent Palestinian-American voice in the United States and its capital, Washington, DC. ATFP's founding aim is to advocate an end to the Palestinian-Israel conflict through the creation of a Palestinian state to live alongside Israel in peace. In the pages of this short volume, the basic ideas promoted by ATFP regarding the path to peace in the Middle East, how to advocate for the creation of a Palestinian state, and ATFP's vision for the nature of the Palestinian state are elaborated and explained.

The title of this volume, "Principles and Pragmatism," reflects the essence of ATFP's approach to its task, a marriage of convictions based on universal moral principles and realistic assessments born of a serious evaluation of politics as the art of the possible. ATFP holds that principles and pragmatism are not opposing forces but actually compliment each other since unrealizable ideological visions are, in fact, illusions that lead to miscalculation and strife. In order to be a genuine force for good in the world, serious principles must be combined with a sober assessment of what can and cannot be accomplished and what in fact will improve the lives of millions of ordinary people. ATFP is not interested in upholding any form of empty rhetoric that gives a political constituency emotional satisfaction while serving in practice as an obstacle to resolving conflicts and bringing hope to peoples who have been mired for decades in bloodshed and oppression.

As explicated at length in this volume, the first principle that underlies ATFP's work is its commitment to the American national interest. ATFP makes its case on the basis of the national interests and goals of US foreign policy, as defined by successive administrations and the foreign policy establishment more broadly including the leadership in Congress. ATFP does not believe that such interests and goals must be redefined, since an end of conflict in the Middle East based on two states is already a clearly stated US foreign policy objective. However, it does argue that improvements in specific US policies could better serve this aim and that achieving it should be among the highest, if not the single most important, of priorities for US foreign policy. ATFP has argued that end of conflict based on the creation of a Palestinian state would enhance the national security of the United States and strike a powerful blow at the ideology of terrorists, improve our ability to promote democracy and other American values in the Middle East and around the world, and provide significant economic opportunities for both Americans and peoples of the region.

This approach to Palestinian-American advocacy that foregrounds the American national interest and the patriotic nature of ATFP as an American organization is a departure from traditional modes of Arab-American and Palestinian-American advocacy, which has all-too-often set itself at odds with national security strategies and foreign policy goals as defined by the US government. This stance reflects both principle, in that ATFP's Board of Directors and staff regard themselves as patriotic Americans concerned first and foremost with the interests of our country, and pragmatism, insofar as any other starting point is unlikely, and for good reason, to be taken seriously by our fellow Americans.

ATFP's commitment to an end of conflict based on two states also reflects a marriage of principle and pragmatism. ATFP advocates a two-state solution because it believes that this is the only viable solution to ending the conflict between Israel and the Palestinians, which would allow both peoples to seek their way forward without enduring an ongoing struggle with no end in sight. ATFP holds that, whatever its flaws, the two-state solution offers the two peoples, the region, and the world the only practicable means of resolving one of the most intractable and politically damaging struggles of our time.

The status quo, with Israel ruling millions of Palestinians who are not citizens of Israel or any other state and large amounts of Palestinian territory beyond the internationally recognized boundaries of Israel, is completely untenable. Israeli unilateralism can only defer a confrontation with the essential issues between the two peoples, and will not end the conflict but only deepen and entrench the divisions and further raise the stakes.

The question of Jerusalem is particularly crucial to resolving the conflict. ATFP holds that Israeli exclusivity in Jerusalem is a recipe for continued conflict with the Palestinians, since a Palestinian state without a sovereign role in occupied East Jerusalem would not be a viable entity. But more dangerous still, Israeli exclusive control of Jerusalem creates the circumstance through which the conflict could easily morph from a difficult but resolvable political struggle between two ethno-national communities over land and power into an even more intractable and possibly irreconcilable religious quarrel. It is a formula for protracted confrontation between Israel and the Muslim world in general.

Among both Israelis and Palestinians, minority discourses demanding complete Israeli/Jewish or Palestinian/Muslim rule over the whole of historical Palestine plainly offer nothing for the future but ongoing and in all likelihood catastrophic conflict and violence without apparent resolution, since neither side can seriously hope for any sort of comprehensive military solution. Neither Israelis nor Palestinians, both of whom exist in roughly equivalent numbers between the river and the sea, are going to vanish from the land, and neither shows the least interest in either accepting subjugation at the hands of the other or in abandoning its respective national identity. Utopian visions of a single, democratic state in which Israelis and Palestinians both set aside their national identities in favor of an as-yet-undefined umbrella identity in some sort of joint or bi-national state may be appealing in their own way, but they do not constitute a serious or practicable path to ending the conflict.

Both of these extremes, whether maximal nationalist visions of exclusive domination by one or the other group in the whole of historical Palestine, or the negation of both Israeli and Palestinian national aspirations in a single, undefined state, are mistakenly understood by their proponents as principled stances. In fact, they represent unworkable fantasies and, in practice, the demand for either of them abandons the goal of resolving the conflict and ending the occupation in favor of an open-ended struggle in pursuit of what would certainly seem to be impossible goals. These maximalist and minimalist visions for the realization of Israeli and Palestinian nationalisms represent neither principle nor pragmatism, and instead reflect dangerous phantasms and fanaticism.

One of the most compelling aspects of the two-state solution is that a solid majority of both Palestinians and Israelis have shown, in virtually every poll taken in the past 20 years and more, that they are in favor of peace based on two states. Moreover, the international community, the UN Security Council, and the international legal framework for addressing the conflict are all very clear in their support for an end of conflict based on the creation of a Palestinian state living alongside Israel in peace. ATFP argues that radical minorities on both sides and in the United States have thus far been able to thwart the mutual wishes of the large majority of both Israelis and Palestinians to live in peace as neighbors in two independent, sovereign states. They have also been allowed to impede the realization of a crucial American national security interest, as articulated by both the Clinton and Bush Administrations.

ATFP promotes the two-state solution from the viewpoint of patriotic American citizens who are committed first and foremost to the best interests of the United States. ATFP sees itself as an American institution, not a Palestinian one. ATFP believes that nothing can be accomplished without working inside the political system and fully embracing our rights and our role as American citizens. As such, it focuses on dealing directly with the US government, and has developed solid working relations with both the executive and legislative branches. ATFP has also reached out to think tanks, the media, educational institutions, and other non-governmental organizations to build a coalition in favor of ending the conflict based on two states. ATFP has argued, as detailed in this volume, that a broad-based alliance needs urgently to be formed that joins the many disparate groups which, for their own reasons, all support this aim but which have never worked together to promote it and sometimes even regarded each other with suspicion and hostility. ATFP holds that support for the two-state solution should bring these groups together, on this one all-important issue if on nothing else, into a working partnership designed to offset supporters of the untenable status quo, and those whose maximalist or minimalist prescriptions for nationalism are a recipe for endless conflict.

ATFP's principled and pragmatic stance is based also on the recognition that both the Israeli and Palestinian peoples have a right to realize their national identities and to exercise sovereignty in the land of historical Palestine. Both are entitled to self-determination, and both have a right to be present where they, in fact, are in the land between the river and the sea. Denying either national community the opportunity to govern itself and fulfill or maintain its national identity through a sovereign, independent state is both a formula for protracted conflict and would constitute a denial of a right recognized for both peoples by international law and numerous UN Security Council resolutions. Beyond this, ATFP has outlined its vision for the Palestinian state, which again reflects both its principles and a pragmatic evaluation of the commitments that would best enable a state to meet the essential needs of the Palestinian people. ATFP, as explicated in this volume, holds that the Palestinian state should be pluralistic, democratic, non-militarized, and neutral. These are principled positions, to be sure, and reflect moral aims that should be striven towards and may, like many moral commitments undertaken by states and societies the world over, never be fully realized. Yet, they would constitute a governing ethos that would give the Palestinians a powerful moral voice within the family of nations and reflect the bitter lessons of their painful history of displacement, dispossession, exile, and occupation. At the same time, ATFP believes that these principles are also pragmatic positions that would strengthen the Palestinian state, provide the best platform for good governance and domestic stability and security, and maximize the role the State of Palestine would play on the world stage. Again, ATFP would argue that principle and pragmatism come together in a realistic assessment of what is possible and what is desirable, and that these supposedly competing values are not only reconcilable but can and should be complimentary.

This volume represents the essence of ATFP's work during its brief history and elaborates the various aspects of principle and pragmatism that have informed its work. ATFP trusts that these ideas will form a lasting contribution to the Palestinian and American dialogues on the conflict in the Middle East and a serious intervention in the quest for freedom and peace.

1. ATFP MISSION STATEMENT

ATFP is a not-for-profit organization that advocates to the American people the national security interests of the United States in establishing a Palestinian state.

Specifically, ATFP seeks to promote the awareness of the far-reaching benefits that Palestinian statehood will have for the US in the following areas: (1) enhancement of national security, as well as regional peace and stability; (2) proliferation of American values of freedom and democracy; and (3) expansion of economic opportunities throughout the Arab and Islamic worlds, resulting from an atmosphere of peace and cooperation.

ATFP advocates the establishment of a democratic state of Palestine living in peace and security alongside Israel in the territories occupied in 1967 in accordance with international law and the relevant United Nations resolutions.

As an organization committed to peace and human rights, ATFP categorically and unequivocally condemns all violence directed against civilians no matter who the victims or perpetrators may be.

ATFP believes that permanent peace in the Middle East, as well as world peace, can only be achieved by a historic compromise based on a two-state solution, with a shared Jerusalem and a just solution for the refugee problem according to international law. This vision of peace has the support of the US government, the UN, the European Community, each member of the Arab League, and the majorities of the Palestinian and Israeli peoples. Nevertheless, despite overwhelming international support, the realization of this vision has yet to materialize in any meaningful way, with continued tragic consequences. It is the goal of ATFP to advance the implementation of the international consensus with alacrity and resolve.

ATFP plans to fulfill this mission of peace by coordinating the efforts of Americans of Palestinian heritage working, with their fellow Americans and others, across the spectrum of civic, educational, cultural, legal, economic, and political fields.

2. SIX PRINCIPLES TOWARDS A FAIR AND LASTING SOLUTION TO THE ISRAELI-PALESTINIAN CONFLICT

ATFP advocates the following six principles towards a fair and lasting solution to the Israeli-Palestinian conflict:

1. Two sovereign states—Israel and Palestine—living side by side in peace and security based on the borders of June 4, 1967 with mutually agreed upon territorial adjustments.

2. An end to the Israeli occupation and the evacuation of all Israeli settlements, save for equitable arrangements mutually agreed upon by the negotiating parties.

3. A just solution for the Palestinian refugee problem, in accordance with international legality and the relevant UN resolutions.

4. A shared Jerusalem open to all faiths, serving as the capital of two states, providing for the fulfillment of the political aspirations of both the Palestinian and Israeli peoples.

5. Full acceptance of Israel by all Arab states, and normalized diplomatic and economic relations throughout the region.

6. A "Marshall Plan" style package of aid and investment for Palestine and the new Middle East.

Palestinian statehood will remove the greatest single source of anti-American sentiment throughout the Arab and Muslim worlds, enhance the security of all states in the Middle East by establishing defined borders for Israel, establish a democratic model for the rest of the Arab world to emulate; and open up substantial markets in the Middle East and North Africa to greater opportunities for economic cooperation.

3. ATFP STATEMENT OF PRINCIPLES ON JERUSALEM

1. A resolution of the issue of Jerusalem can only come about through direct negotiations between Israeli and Palestinian officials as an expression of their national policies. No other parties are entitled to negotiate on this issue.

2. Jerusalem is a central part of the present and futures of both Palestinian and Israeli societies, and is holy to Jews, Christians, and Muslims around the world. Lasting peace can only be achieved by securing the political aspirations of both peoples and the religious rights of the three religions.

3. There can be no monopoly of sovereignty by either party. Jerusalem should remain shared and undivided. The occupation of Arab East Jerusalem must end and it should serve as the capital of the future State of Palestine. West Jerusalem should serve as the capital of Israel.

4. No religion or nationality can be privileged in Jerusalem. The right of access to holy places and the right of worship in the city must be guaranteed for people of all faiths from around the world.

5. Unilateral measures taken by Israel since 1967 and that continue until today, cannot be allowed to dictate or prejudice the final status of Jerusalem. Such measures include buildings, confiscation of land, barriers and walls, as well as political and legal documents.

Selected Jerusalem Facts:

- There have been 11 Security Council resolutions since 1967 critical of Israeli activities changing the status of Jerusalem. The Security Council has repeatedly declared that all measures taken by Israel to change the demographic composition, physical character, institutional structure, or status of occupied territories, including Jerusalem, are null and void (Resolutions 446, 425, 465).

- There are 211,000 Israeli settlers in East Jerusalem living in 15 settlements

- 66% of what Israel has declared to be "united" Jerusalem today is territory seized by force: 5% comprises the old Jordanian municipality while 61% is West Bank territory added to the expanded Jerusalem municipal border following the June 1967 war, approximately 17,500 acres.

- Approximately 230,000 Palestinians hold East Jerusalem residency permits. About 60,000 of these people are located on the West Bank side of the barrier and will need Israeli permission to cross the barrier to access services to which they are entitled inside Jerusalem.

4. ATFP STATEMENT OF PRINCIPLES ON THE PALESTINIAN REFUGEE ISSUE

1. A resolution of the Palestinian refugee issue can only come about through direct negotiations between Israeli and Palestinian officials as an expression of their national policies. No other parties are entitled to negotiate on this issue. However, individuals and organizations are free to express their opinions on this issue in the spirit of free, open, and respectful debate.

2. There are many parties responsible for the suffering of the Palestinian refugees. Responsible parties include first Israel for displacing the Palestinian refugees, refusing their return, and confiscating their property without compensation. Some Arab states also bear varying degrees of responsibility; some for allowing generations of refugees to languish in camps under miserable conditions, or by placing various restrictions in terms of their legal status, employment, and travel rights, and others for not having done enough to ease the suffering of refugees. Finally, the Palestinian leadership has been at fault for not communicating honestly and openly with the refugees on what they can expect for their future.

3. The right of return is an integral part of international humanitarian law, and cannot be renounced by any parties. There is no Palestinian constituency of consequence that would agree to the renunciation of this right. There is also no Jewish constituency of consequence in Israel that would accept the return of millions of Palestinian refugees.

4. Although the right of return cannot be renounced, it should not stand in the way of the only identifiable peaceful prospect for ending the Israeli-Palestinian conflict: a resolution based on a State of Israel living side-by-side with a Palestinian state in the occupied territories with its capital in East Jerusalem. Implementation of the right of return cannot obviate the logic of a resolution based on two states. The challenge for the Israeli and Palestinian national leaderships is to arrive at a formula that recognizes refugee rights but which does not contradict the basis of a two-state solution and an end to the conflict.

5. As part of any comprehensive settlement ending the conflict, Israel should accept its moral responsibility to apologize to the Palestinian people for the creation of the refugee problem. Palestinians should accept that this acknowledgment of responsibility does not undermine the legitimacy of present-day Israel.

5. A VISION FOR THE STATE OF PALESTINE: The Nature and Character of the State[1]

Introduction

The core mission of the American Task Force on Palestine (ATFP) is to promote the creation of Palestine to live alongside Israel in peace. ATFP believes that now is the time for proponents of the creation of a Palestinian state to articulate in detail their vision of the nature and character of that state. ATFP has drafted this document to outline its vision for Palestine, strongly feeling that independence from occupation is not an end in itself and that statehood should provide the means to truly liberate the Palestinian people and restore their national dignity.

ATFP advocates the fulfillment of Palestinian national aspirations for a politically viable Palestinian state in the West Bank and Gaza Strip, with its capital in Arab East Jerusalem. ATFP holds that this is the only workable option for ending the conflict between Israel and the Palestinian people. Palestine must be politically viable, in that it should fulfill the legitimate national aspirations of the Palestinian people for independence and self-determination. Its creation must represent not simply peace as an absence of war, but an end to the conflict between Israel and other states and peoples in the Middle East.

Palestine should also fulfill its promise of becoming a new democracy in the family of nations, indeed a model of democracy for other regional states, as well as a partner for peace to Israel and a friend of the US in the Middle East. It should provide the Palestinian people with a renewed sense of national dignity and national service, and the ability to participate in the full range of political processes at the domestic, regional, and international levels.

Palestine should be pluralistic and democratic with equal rights, including equal opportunities, for all its citizens. It should enact and uphold laws that facilitate and regulate open trade and encourage global investment. ATFP strongly advocates that Palestine aspire to play a positive, stabilizing role in the region, and earnestly hopes that it will join the small group of states that deliberately choose the path of non-militarization. ATFP also urges that the values espoused in this vision should be at the core of the curriculum for educating future generations of Palestinians.

---

[1] ATFP statement first published in *The New York Times*, February 3, 2006.

I. Territorial Boundaries, Jerusalem, and Refugees

The territorial boundaries of Palestine will be determined by negotiators representing the elected governments of Israel and the Palestinian people, respectively. It is not the role of an organization such as ATFP to draw lines on maps or dictate to national leaderships on matters to be determined through negotiation. However, ATFP supports the principle stated in the Roadmap of the Quartet and in several United Nations resolutions, of creating a state of Palestine alongside Israel by ending the Israeli occupation that began in 1967. ATFP supports the position articulated by US President George W. Bush in 2005 that any adjustments to the armistice lines of 1949 must be mutually agreed upon.

Palestine must be a fully sovereign member state of the UN, with jurisdiction over the West Bank and Gaza Strip and its capital in Arab East Jerusalem. In order for Palestine to be acceptable to Palestinians, it must be contiguous within the West Bank. Clearly, a major transportation route for safe passage of people and goods between the West Bank and the Gaza Strip is an essential requirement. A viable Palestine should have complete control over its territory, airspace, borders, territorial waters, electro-magnetic spectrum, and fresh water and other natural resources.

Jerusalem is a central part of the present and futures of both Palestinian and Israeli societies, and is holy to Jews, Christians, and Muslims around the world. For this reason, ATFP has long argued that there can be no monopoly of sovereignty in Jerusalem, which should remain shared and undivided.

The viability of Palestine would be fatally undermined if Palestinian society were cut off from its social, cultural, religious, educational, and economic center in Arab East Jerusalem. Without a reasonable compromise on Jerusalem respecting the rights of both peoples and all three faiths, the national political conflict between Israel and the Palestinians over land and sovereignty could be increasingly supplanted by a religious conflict that will last for decades to come.

Arab East Jerusalem should serve as the capital of the independent state of Palestine while West Jerusalem would serve as the capital of Israel. ATFP advocates a united and shared city with an integrated municipality thus allowing it to function as a modern city, a political capital for both Palestine and Israel, and a spiritual capital for Muslims, Christians, and Jews.

Palestine should serve as a haven for Palestinian refugees from around the Middle East and the rest of the world. Negotiations between the elected leaderships of Israel and the Palestinian people will have to arrive at a mutually agreed solution for implementing the rights of the refugees for return and compensation, as outlined in UN Resolution 194. Whatever the outcome of these negotiations, Palestine should open its doors to refugees from around the region and stand prepared to provide various forms of vital assistance to Palestinians wherever they may be.

II. Character of Palestine

1. Pluralistic

The Palestinian people have emerged from their traumatic recent history as a distinct national community within the broader Arab cultural framework. They are united by their shared experience, largely defined in terms of the conflict with Israel, and other distinctly Palestinian sources of cultural and political identity. They are also united in their aspiration for an end to the occupation and the establishment of a state in Palestine that can realize their long-denied fundamental human and national rights.

However, within the context of that essential unity there lies a great diversity of affiliations and sub-national identities. Palestinians include a variety of religious orientations, including numerous Muslim and Christian denominations and sects. Some Palestinians trace their family origins to many parts of the Arab and Mediterranean worlds, and beyond. Developing as they have from a place of migration, pilgrimage, warfare, and trade for millennia, Palestinians reflect a vast diversity of influences and ancestries. There also exists a wide spectrum of ideological, educational, and economic diversity among Palestinians, from the socialist left to the religious right. And, of course, Palestinian society also incorporates the universal national distinctions of regional differences, between urban and rural communities and among various social classes.

Palestine not only must accommodate these differences, it should embrace them. The formal structures of democracy, as many historical experiences have demonstrated, are not in and of themselves a guarantee of pluralism, in which all citizens have an equal opportunity to participate in the civil, political, cultural, and economic life of the society. Palestine should be built on a set of commitments to empowering all of its citizens and, from the outset, deliberately foster an ethos of inclusiveness and acceptance within the national community. Palestine should be a state for all its citizens, with citizenship being the only basis for inclusion in the national community.

Palestine should set a new standard in the Middle East wherein the state shows due regard for the rights of each and every individual, not just inasmuch as they participate in the collectivities of the Palestinian state and society, but also on the grounds of their inviolable rights as individual human beings. Its people will be among the major resources of Palestine. Palestine must base its future development on human capital and the careful cultivation of human resources. The positive experiences of certain post-colonial states in East Asia, which are relatively small and poor in natural resources but have emphasized education and citizen empowerment, could be seen as a developmental model for Palestine.

Pluralism—that accommodates the widest possible variety of choices for the Palestinian people and embraces cultural, economic, religious, social, and political differences—is an essential element in paving the way for Palestine to become a society based on the cultivation of its powerful latent human capital. In particular, the enhancement and protection of children's and women's rights are essential to this national strategy. The right of people to live their lives with a maximum of autonomy, freedom, and protection from discrimination is the sine qua non of genuine independence and true liberation. In this regard, the legal and constitutional commitments for the protection of individual, women's, and minority rights made by post-Apartheid South Africa should be carefully studied.

Faith and religion have played, and will continue to play, an invaluable defining role in the lives and culture of the people of Palestine. However, a pluralistic state in a heterogeneous society (and virtually all national societies are, in fact, heterogeneous) must be a secular state, in the sense that the government remains strictly neutral on matters of religion. The state may invoke or embody certain religious values, but it cannot interfere with the free exercise of religion, mandate a state religion to be followed by the public at large, or enact laws and restrictions favoring one creed or another. If the state adopts any of these practices, religious discrimination is inevitable. Such discrimination is antithetical to the principles of equality and social pluralism, especially where religious differences in a society are well established and obvious. The Middle East, including Israel and many Arab states, is a region rife with religious passions and governments that invoke and manipulate sectarian religious sentiments and prejudices. Palestine must not fall into this same pattern of religious privilege and discrimination. It must be a genuinely pluralistic state for all its citizens, which recognizes and celebrates their diversity while it treats them equally and with neutrality. This is only possible in a secular political system.

2. Democratic

Palestine, for reasons of its own internal stability and for the regional role it needs to play, should be a democratic state built on the foundations of pluralism. Its political structures will be based on a multiparty system without ideological disqualifiers, that regular elections ensure the consent of the governed, that there be an independent judiciary that applies the rule of law in an equitable and impartial manner, and that fundamental individual political rights such as freedom of expression and assembly are guaranteed.

The credibility of the state as the embodiment of the national aspirations of the Palestinian people depends not only on the trappings of sovereignty, but also on the direct empowerment of ordinary Palestinians through the electoral and broader political process. Palestinians, whose cause is widely and passionately advocated around the world, will have a unique opportunity to build a genuinely democratic constitutional republic. They should avoid the common failings of parts of the Arab world as they strive to provide a model for others to emulate. Palestine must not be perceived as representing a single party dictatorship, an oligarchy of the wealthy, or a kleptocracy of the powerful. It must provide its citizens the political structures and institutions that afford them the necessary means to pursue political agendas, change, and reform.

For democracy to work in Palestine, all major factions, including opposition groups, will have to agree to play by the same rules and uphold the same law. This means no entity other than the state can legitimately employ force in Palestine, and that it will do so through national institutions that shall remain politically neutral and respect the peaceful transfer of power through fair and legitimate elections. It means that the state will have a strict monopoly on security forces and lawful arms subject to oversight by an independent court system and an elected legislature. It means that all parties are expected to commit not only to participating in, but also maintaining, the democratic structures of the state. The rule of law is critical in establishing a bulwark against any individuals or groups that would seek to reduce Palestinian democracy to its formal trappings by establishing what amounts to a single party system, or those who would seek victory in elections with the intention of ultimately limiting which individuals and groups can or cannot participate in future elections. Democratic constitutional structures should be protected from easy and swift change based on any single election result or the passions of a given moment.

The Palestinian people and their society are well-placed to establish a fully realized democratic political system in an independent state. The presidential and legislative elections in January 2005 and 2006 were successfully held in spite of the difficulties of life under military occupation and limited external support. Nonetheless, a competitive, multiparty campaign was conducted, and the elections were certified free and fair by all international observers.

These elections were the result of decades of political developments among Palestinians, which have laid the groundwork for a culture of democracy. They strongly suggest that Palestinians have independently arrived at a political culture that embodies a nascent democracy, and that such elections could be repeated on a regular basis. It should be understood that such lofty goals will not be achievable instantaneously, but will require years of dedicated and delicate effort by Palestinians, their neighbors, and the international community to develop fully-realized democratic structures in Palestine. No state ever completely lives up to the goals it sets itself for justice, transparency, the rule of law, and other markers of democratic order. However democratic states establish institutions that remain loyal to, and continue to strive to accomplish, these goals. Deficiencies and setbacks must not be allowed to undermine a broad commitment to democratic processes and goals if those principles are ever to be fully realized.

Palestinians have a promising start from which to develop politically, but a fully functional democracy in Palestine will require not only the realization of independence, but also significant support from the outside world. Governments, international institutions, and nongovernmental organizations from around the world can be of great help over time in assisting the Palestinian people and government to build a democratic political system. A democratic Palestine would not only be a partner in peace with Israel and a friend of the US, it would also be a model for other regional states to follow.

3. Non-militarized

The Palestinian people should strongly consider creating a non-militarized state. This means relying on a politically neutral National Guard for internal stability and law and order, and Border Guard for securing places of ingress and egress to the territory of the state, but not maintaining a standing army. Palestine is a small country that will be divided into two parts (the West Bank and Gaza Strip). It will not be able to prevail in armed conflict with any of its neighbors.

Its internal stability can, and should only, be insured by a robust, politically neutral National Guard, which could provide all services needed by the Palestinian people in the event of their independence. The National Guard should, through its composition and demeanor, foster a valuable sense of dignity and national service. The immediate order of business in the independent state of Palestine must be social and economic development. Non-militarization would realize very substantial economic benefits and free resources for investment in education and other tools for the development of human capital, which should be the foremost priority.

The bedrock for a secure Palestine should be a treaty of protection with NATO, compatible with membership in the Arab League, to ensure that the territorial integrity of the state is never violated by any party. In past negotiations, the Palestinians have suggested they would not object to such protection for Israel as well, to ensure that neither Palestine nor Israel would ever be subject to attacks, as well as to ensure that Israel would never be tempted to re-occupy Palestine. These international security guarantees would be the most fundamental step the international community could take to ensure peace and stability in the region and they should be codified in UN resolutions.

4. A Positive, Stabilizing Regional Player

As a complement to a policy of non-militarization, ATFP believes that Palestine should strive to serve as a positive, stabilizing actor in the region. The Palestinian people, having endured warfare, occupation, dispossession, and exile for most of the past century, have nothing to gain by becoming entangled in any conflicts they can possibly avoid. Palestine should embody a culture that rejects warfare as a means of resolving international disputes and promotes instead multilateralism and an adherence to international law.

The Palestinian experience, more than most others, attests to the futility of attempts to settle differences between peoples through violence and to the urgent need to create a system of international legality that protects all people actively and impartially. A Palestinian state committed to peaceful coexistence, non-belligerence and military neutrality would have a powerful moral voice in promoting international legality and regional stability.

Palestine can further contribute to regional stability by establishing and upholding policies and laws that facilitate and regulate open trade with all its neighbors, and encourage investment and partnership from around the globe.

ATFP offers this vision of the anticipated and promising state of Palestine as a lasting contribution to the Palestinian national debate, an outline of a state that can serve the fundamental needs of the Palestinian people and that would be a positive, stabilizing actor in the region and an important ethical presence in the family of nations.

6. STRATEGIES FOR ADVOCATING PALESTINIAN STATEHOOD

*A document outlining ATFP's approach
to advocacy for peace based on two states*

The following represents the analysis of the American Task Force on Palestine (ATFP) on the most effective strategies in the American political context for advocating an end to the Israeli occupation and the creation of a Palestinian state with its capital in East Jerusalem. It serves as a guide to AFTP's own advocacy on behalf of Palestine, and is also offered as advice to all those who wish to successfully advocate for Palestinian statehood in the context of a two-state solution in the Middle East.

Advocacy for Palestine in the US should be guided by one main objective: to have a positive impact on government policy and decision-making. Almost 60 years of traditional pro-Palestinian advocacy in the US, largely aimed at making the case against Israel, has simply failed to yield a satisfactory outcome. Existing strategies have not succeeded in engendering any broad sympathy and identification in the American public for the Palestinian people, and have failed to produce or support alterations to US foreign policy. We must therefore re-examine our assumptions as we formulate a strategy aimed at achieving policy changes rather than merely scoring debating points. Our advocacy should emphasize the positive aspects of Palestinian statehood, and especially why the creation of a Palestinian state is good for the US. Pro-Palestinian events, public relations campaigns, public education efforts, and other measures aimed at persuading the American public that the occupation must end and lead to the creation of a Palestinian state should stress the reasonable message that US foreign policy should be balanced and fair, and oriented towards the accomplishment of a viable and achievable peace. Of course, criticism of Israeli policies, especially when it is warranted (such as in the case of settlement activity, the West Bank barrier, unilateral measures that prejudice final status outcomes, the closure regime, economic warfare, the use of military force, assassinations and torture, and so forth) plainly needs to be an important part of the discourse. Moreover, criticism of Palestinian state and non-state actors should also be included in the arguments, as warranted. But the focus must always be on the positive effects of the creation of a Palestinian state for the US, as well as the peoples of the region.

Above all, the debate about this issue, and other foreign policy matters, in the US is an American debate. Participants cannot be, or be perceived to be, foreign, let alone anti-American. Opposition to government policy, including foreign policies, is not only possible, but is built into the

American political system. Although what is perceived as constructive and patriotic criticism of US foreign policy is perfectly legitimate, no arguments or set of ideas stand a chance of political success, or even becoming a serious part of the national conversation if they are perceived as alien, unpatriotic, or constructed in the service of foreign agenda. Given present political realities in the US, Arab-American, and even American Muslim, organizations have a particular need to avoid being perceived as representing politically unassimilated immigrants who cling to imported politics that reflect sensibilities and allegiances shaped in the Middle East. Historically, the Arab-American community has established few political alliances in the US and has been commonly viewed, whether fairly or unfairly, as less "genuinely American" than other ethnic group organizations. They have not worked effectively within the American political system, and have not presented the Palestinian case with an American face.

Partly as a consequence of these failures, a majority of the American public, as well as the political establishment, have developed only limited sympathy towards the Palestinians, even though the country officially endorses a Palestinian state. The problem is not just that the American political establishment, with the backing of the public, is well disposed towards the defense of Israel, regardless of whether they approve of all aspects of Israeli policy. It is also that the seemingly strident and critical rhetoric that has characterized most previous pro-Palestinian advocacy efforts misleadingly suggest the Palestinians are motivated more by an antipathy towards Israel and the US than being committed to their own national liberation and statehood. The Palestinian national movement can define itself best if it seeks positive, pro-active change that embraces freedom, liberation, and democracy in the establishment of its own viable state. For the Palestinian movement to be perceived as simply critical of or "anti" Israel without communicating any significant positive content, condemns it to a cold and unenthusiastic reception by most Americans, who are looking for a solution to, rather than an explanation of, the conflict. The most sophisticated research into US public opinion strongly suggests that most Americans are far more interested in constructive ideas about, and hearing a commitment to, resolving the conflict, than they are in listening to heart-rending narratives or historical grievances, whether Arab or Jewish.

The ATFP Strategy for Pro-Palestinian Advocacy

ATFP argues that Palestinian Americans and other American supporters of their cause should make full use of their citizenship as Americans in reaching out to its audience. A crucial factor in the success of other American ethnic groups in influencing American foreign policy has been to emphasize the patriotic nature of this advocacy. Jewish Americans, Cubans, Irish, Greeks, Armenians, Iraqis, and other ethnic groups in the US that have sought to influence foreign policy to their own ends have all done so by framing their arguments primarily in terms of the US national interest. To be sure, all policy positions require a moral basis, and the justice of the Palestinian cause and the tragedy of the Palestinian narrative are essential elements to any program of successful advocacy for Palestine. Nonetheless, the first question Americans want answered is: How is this important to our country? Unfortunately, Palestinian Americans and their supporters have often been exceptionally poor at articulating an answer to this question, and usually do not even attempt to do so. Instead, pro-Palestinian advocacy in the US has typically focused on denunciations of American support for Israel, which, though justified, have at times been strident enough to sound like overt anti-Americanism. This is all the more unfortunate given the obvious and powerful arguments Palestinians can deploy in advocating for an American national interest in creating a Palestinian state. In essence, we must argue that American interests are served by supporting the morally just goal of Palestinian independence and ending the occupation; that Americans can, as the saying goes, "do well by doing good" not in some abstract sense, but simply by applying the logic of the existing goals and strategies for US foreign policy in the Middle East articulated by the Administration and accepted by most of the rest of the American political establishment.

These arguments can roughly be summarized in the five following points:

1. **Promote General US Interests in the Middle East**. Peace based on the creation of a Palestinian state will remove the greatest single obstacle to achieving US policy objectives in the Middle East. Every poll, study, and survey of Middle Eastern, and specifically Arab, public opinion since the start of the second Intifada in September 2000 has demonstrated the profoundly negative effect that this conflict has had on Arab perceptions of the US. This negative opinion cuts across national, class, religious, geographical, and other barriers, and is widely recognized as a major problem in Washington and by Americans. It is a fairly non-controversial view, although infrequently argued, that the simplest and most profound gesture to repair the US image among the Arabs would be for the US to take a leading role in resolving the Palestinian-Israeli conflict and help the Palestinians achieve freedom and independence. It is even understood that this would influence positively events in Iraq, and beyond. More specifically, the emerging Palestinian state will be a new democracy, a new ally of the US, and a peace partner to Israel.

2. **Remove one of the Major Rallying Calls of Terrorists.** Most observers have agreed, and most Americans have accepted, that the militant Islamist movements have more or less hijacked the Palestinian cause, and that the suffering of the Palestinians and the persistence of the conflict constitutes a major rhetorical device that allows them to pursue recruits and support for anti-American violent activity. Many people, including former senior government officials, CIA officers, political scientists and commentators, and others closely associated with the American political establishment have made the point forcefully that a resolution of the conflict and the creation of a Palestinian state would be a major blow against anti-American extremism in the region. In essence, the argument is that creating a State of Palestine makes America more secure. Advocates for Palestine also have to be consistent, and leave no room for ambiguity, about their total and uncompromising opposition to terrorism, and all violence against civilians no matter what the cause, or who the perpetrators or victims, might be.

3. **Enhance the US Role as World Leader.** Americans are aware that they have assumed the role of "world leadership' and have the sense that this presently involves the cooperation of established powers such as the European Union, Japan and Russia, as well as emerging powers such as India, China, and Brazil. A powerful argument can be made that resolving the longest running and most politically divisive conflicts in the world would be an important demonstration of the responsibility and worthiness of US in its role as 'world leader.' It would be an enormous enhancement both to the stature and legacy of any individual American political figure who could take credit for this achievement, and to the international standing of the US. It would greatly reduce perceptions that the US operates a system of double standards, and show that the US is capable of providing benefits to Arabs generally and to Palestinians in particular. It would also support the argument that the US is a force for international law and order, rather than one that enforces UN Security Council resolutions in an arbitrary and self-interested manner.

4. **Open Major Middle Eastern Economic Markets.** Many economists have suggested that US economic interests have been held back across the Middle East because of skepticism and hostility resulting largely from the Palestinian-Israeli conflict. This limited trade to the region, mostly to oil and its products. Resolving the conflict would mean the removal of major barriers to trade and other relations between the US and 22 Arab states, and 1.2 billion Muslims around the world, to the tremendous mutual benefit of both Americans and Arabs. Resolution of this damaging conflict would lead to enhanced US bilateral commercial ties with 56 Muslim countries with an enormous windfall for the American economy and for the economy and standard of living of people of all these countries.

5. **Promote American Values Worldwide.** The creation of a Palestinian state corresponds to the most stated fundamental American political values of freedom, independence, and democracy. Americans need to be educated repeatedly about the fact that the 3.5 million Palestinians living under Israeli occupation are the largest group of non-citizens in the world today. Americans have a profound sense, which can be tapped into with enormous effect, of the rights and responsibilities of citizenship. In order to promote an understanding that the key to peace is an end to the occupation, it must be made clear that occupation means living without citizenship and under a government to which one has no access and in which one is totally unrepresented. The Palestinians are a well-educated people with a thriving internal civil society and a history of political pluralism, and there is little doubt that democracy will be able to take root among them if they are independent. Therefore, establishing a Palestinian state means the birth of a genuine democracy, and the emergence of millions of new citizens of a new democracy, and the ending of a period in which millions of people lived without benefit of those basic political freedoms that constitute the founding ethos of the US.

ATFP believes that in pro-Palestinian advocacy in the US, the idea of "establishing a Palestinian state" should always be yoked to the concept of "living alongside Israel in peace." This completes the circle by emphasizing that the goal is peace, and removes any doubts about intentions of the Palestinian national movement vis-à-vis the future of Israel. This is important because advocates representing the Israeli right have been successful in painting the Palestinian movement as being driven to criticize, attack, and even destroy Israel, rather than to create freedom and independence for the Palestinian people and to accomplish reconciliation and an end to the conflict. As noted above, common tactics employed by pro-Palestinian rhetoric in US have played into this misperception by concentrating energy on criticizing Israel and either downplaying or leaving out altogether the positive content of regarding the creation of a Palestinian state.

The themes to be stressed are three:
1. *Freedom* for the Palestinians.
2. *Peace* for Israel and all countries in the region.
3. Enhanced *National Security* for the US.

Any policy that promises freedom, peace, and national security will resonate with Americans. The message ATFP will be sending, and urges others to also adopt, can be boiled down into this sentence:

The founding of a Palestinian state to live in peace alongside Israel will mean freedom for the Palestinians, peace for Israel, and enhanced national security for the US.

We are advocating that Palestinian Americans and their supporters should speak *as Americans first*, and emphasize the benefits to the US of the creation of a Palestinian state, rather than emphasizing a strident critique of American foreign policy that sounds accusatory against the US, or by enumerating endlessly the sins of Israel. By doing so, we can maximize our effectiveness and better serve the aim of promoting to Americans the creation of a Palestinian state and an end to the occupation. Our goal is to help create a Palestine that is a strategic ally of the US and a partner to Israel in peace.

7. ON CONSENSUS AND ALLIANCE

Speech by Ziad Asali, delivered at the Union of Progressive Zionists student conference in Newark, New Jersey on October 18, 2004

A consensus, that is, nearly a consensus, about the contours of the final agreement for a genuine and lasting peace is known. It is a variation of the themes of Clinton's Taba proposal, The Geneva Initiative, Nusseibeh-Ayalon, One Voice, and most recently, the Road Map. Polls and surveys of Palestinians, Israelis, American Jews and Arabs, as well as the general American public, indicate support for a two-state solution based on what has come to be called the 'Historic Compromise.' An opposing minority in each camp has exercised its power decisively, predictably and effectively to derail and frustrate a peaceful solution. It has thwarted the will of the majority of all these constituents.

The consensus is so accepted that even the most hardened opponents of the compromise have adopted it publicly, as they worked to obstruct it, in the hope of killing it in due time.

The forces opposed to a two-state solution are opposed to peace at this time because they think that time is on their side. The Israeli opposition, whether national or religious, is based on a claim for Eretz Israel or land of Greater Israel. It believes that if Israel hangs tough it will in time rule most of, if not the whole, land of Palestine, and the Arabs and Muslim will eventually relent and move on to other issues. The Palestinian and Arab opposition, whether national or religious, believes that Israel is just another Crusade that will, in time, perhaps a century or two, be wiped out by the might of a united Muslim power that will liberate Jerusalem again.

The most recent formula for non-peace is the one calling for a bi-national state, a one-state solution, because irreversible facts on the grounds have already precluded the emergence of a viable Palestine. This view does not distinguish between settlements, which can stay, and settlers, who should go back to their country as part of the 'Historic Compromise.' Advocates of this position, which is not in accord with the international consensus, must think that Israel will accede peacefully to the dissolution of its Jewish character after the millennial struggle of the Jewish people to achieve it. We are all waiting with baited breath to see whether there will be support for this formula amongst the Israelis and American Jews. The waiting period will not be one of peace.

Palestinians struggling alone in Palestine can never regain a state in Palestine no matter how heroic, or even wise, they might be. Indeed, even with the support of the whole Arab and Muslims worlds, the Palestinians have been, and will be, unable to achieve independence. An alliance of Palestinians committed to the grand compromise, with significant segments of the Israeli society, working in tandem with Palestinian Americans, other Arab Americans and American Jews, can form the core of the needed alliance to impact policy. The existing global consensus for peace should help empower this alliance to achieve its objective.

Israelis at this point in time, beleaguered, powerful, and defiant, have to make a choice between signing on with the more beleaguered and weakened Palestinians, the majority of whom are anxious to negotiate an end to occupation on very reasonable terms, or to dash the hope of the Palestinians for a state and wait for a less troubling future. Should the compromise fail, it is hard to see how Israel can escape a looming confrontation with over a billion Muslims clamoring for the liberation of Jerusalem for the balance of the century. All in all, this is no prescription for peace.

Why has the minority thwarted peace? The answer is because it could. Why has the majority failed to impose its will for peace? The answer is because it could not. To translate the policy of the majority into political clout is the challenge of our time.

I will spare you the tedium of dwelling on the past. Instead I will try to discuss some issues in American politics that I believe to be relevant, and see how we can learn from them in order to move forward, to achieve our collective goal of genuine peace.

American politics is based on building alliances. It is pluralistic. No single party or group is powerful enough to achieve its objectives on its own. Single issue-oriented alliances are forged between groups pursuing a defined objective that they have in common, regardless of their other strategies, ideologies, or even competing interests. The alliance that traditional Zionists have put in place over decades is awe inspiring in its breadth and depth. Centering on support for Israel, it consisted of groups as varied as the Republican and Democratic parties, labor unions and chambers of commerce, Christian fundamentalists and white liberals, black leaders and conservative southerners, as well as a legion of voices in liberal and conservative media outlets. This alliance is decidedly one of the most successful convergences of strange bedfellows that have ever been assembled. It held together not just to support Israel proper, but also its conquests after 1967.

Another example of a group working on foreign policy issues with measurable success was the obscure Sudan People's Liberation

Movement, a Marxist-Leninist movement established a quarter century ago with a political base in Marxist Ethiopia. Shortly thereafter, a coup in Ethiopia that toppled the regime, orphaned the movement, and forced it to look for a base elsewhere, so it shrewdly moved its political operation to the US. Methodically and successfully, it distanced itself from its ideological past and was able to forge an amazing alliance of Christian fundamentalists, white Christian and Jewish liberals, the Black Caucus and academia with sympathetic media coverage. Yet another successful alliance of disparate groups, with little in common, but with a clear convergence of support for a single goal.

What can we learn from this? One lesson is that there are no quick fixes and no substitute for hard work, and another is that we have to forge ahead and build our own alliance for peace in Palestine/Israel. A cursory look around this country reveals wide support for a two-state solution among the majority of American Jews, particularly those who do not belong to organizations, Arab-, and especially Palestinian-Americans, the moderate wing of the Republican Party, and the progressive wing of the Democratic Party, the public at large, academia, main stream churches, and many ethnic groups with an emerging voice of support in the media. There is no thread that ties these groups together around this issue at this point in time. Indeed, gatherings of like-minded Jewish, and Arab or Palestinian Americans, presumably the core constituents of such an alliance, reveal, more often than not, vast psychological and emotional canyons separating them. Human bonds are rarely created, and tribal links prove to be more solid than reasoned strategies. Real, no-nonsense, business-like communication has yet to evolve.

In the meantime, calm and rational public discourse is stifled by loud, passionate, and personal voices of recrimination and paranoia. These voices have for decades appealed successfully to the core of their communities' insecurities, fears, sense of humiliation, superiority, or inferiority. All these factors made public communication an arena for recrimination and calumny. Individuals could, and did, defy this communal separation at their own risk. To be a non-racist, for a Jew, a Palestinian or any other Arab, and to act like one, is still an act of courage that carries little reward amongst one's peers This communal failure can only be confronted and ameliorated by having more public encounters of concerned people, of equal standing, discussing issues bequeathed by an unkind history, with seriousness and mutual respect. The two communities should endeavor to search for answers rather than to score debating points.

At the risk of offending some, I feel compelled to say that the alliance we seek can only work if it is perceived to serve the interest of each group as they themselves define this interest. Right wing and left wing Jews and Palestinians, here and there, might, for diametrically opposed reasons, agree on the desirability of a two-state solution. This agreement alone makes them eligible potential allies.

The national interest of the US has to be the overarching incentive for forging an effective and wide alliance in our country to support this objective. This interest is best defined, at this age of terrorism and global instability, by the major contribution the resolution of this conflict will make in the Arab and Muslim world towards dissipating the hostility engendered against us; a hostility that has been fully exploited by the Bin Ladens of this world to recruit terrorists and misguided youth.

Palestine, after its independence, can in theory lend itself to the creation of a constitutional, democratic, transparent, and free state. It has the educated human capital to fulfill this promise and it lacks the dictatorial state structure that stifles institution-building in other Arab countries. Constructing such a vibrant state would be consistent with our values and morality. This is yet another argument that will appeal to all people who value freedom in our country.

Clearing the deck of the Palestine/Israel conflict should unlock many artificial political barriers to free trade in the Middle East and would throw the door open for our goods, products and services to a market of three hundred million Arabs, as well as 1.2 billion Muslims. The stunted current trade with all these countries, virtually restricted to oil, will create huge business opportunities in markets that have money and are in need of development—a great fit for our economy. This yet is another argument to help build an enduring and sustainable alliance.

In short, if we are serious about achieving a solution of Palestine-alongside-Israel, we ourselves will have to go about forging the alliance that will make it happen. At the core of it is a self respecting, dependable relationship between Palestinians and Jews in this country and among like-minded people in Palestine and Israel. Anti-Semitism, anti-Arabism, and anti-Islamism are a plague and to be avoided as such. It is our obligation to replace all these ills by a working bond of brave people committed to building an alliance for a genuine and lasting peace.

8. THE TRANSFORMATION OF PALESTINIAN POLITICAL CULTURE

Essay by Ziad Asali, first published in the Jordan Times, December 27, 2005

The political culture in Palestine and the Arab world was defined in the 20th century by the unifying principle of Arab nationalism, which was anti-Western, anti-colonialist and anti-imperialist, and Islamic without being religious, adhering mostly to pragmatic and secular principles. By mid-century, Palestinian and Arab political culture also became clearly anti-Zionist and anti-Arab regimes. These attributes also defined the parameters of political correctness in the Arab world for decades and still hold true today. The crushing military defeat of 1967 at the hands of Israel, the fall of the Soviet Union, and the emergence of political Islam, while virtually decimating Arab nationalism, have made little change in the political culture, including the Palestinian one, that identified the West as its principal adversary.

The past 20 years have seen the rise of a new force in the Arab and Islamic world; militant political Islam. Less sophisticated as a unifying principle than Arab nationalism, it is deeply rooted in Islamic history as a source of legitimacy. It has gradually gained clout, with its extreme elements emboldened by engaging in acts of violence against Western, Arab, and Muslim targets. The new Islamic militants differ from the nationalists in their lack of respect for the principles of secularism, and the-less-than equal status they afford to women and to minorities, yet share an opposition to the West, Zionism, and Arab regimes. However, they have yet to achieve the same status of legitimacy and respectability that Arab nationalism has enjoyed amongst the cultural and intellectual elite.

Today, the generic "Arab Regime" is led by an autocrat and his leading family heading a pyramid of a connected official entourage in charge of the bureaucracy. The political elite is in partnership with a business and military elite based on a simple contract: bribes in lieu of taxes. It is a win-win proposition with the loser being the public that is denied the services of a functioning government and the stability generated by the presence of a broad-based middle class. The fundamental tools of this bargain are the denial of freedom and the suppression of opposition, resulting in a public resentful of its denial of political rights, basic economic opportunities, and benefits of the rule of law. Absence of freedom of expression has left the mosques as the only public venues left open for opposition. In time, and with political skills honed over decades, this opening was fully utilized to generate a militant and absolutist Islamist opposition.

For decades, autocratic Arab regimes with tacit or overt support from the US that shared their interest in stability, have denied political participation to their people and have reaped a cauldron of instability with expanding global implications. Secretary of State Condoleezza Rice has acknowledged the shortcomings of past policy as she compared it to the new Bush policy of restoring a stability based on the consent and the participation of the governed. The success of this policy will depend on the ability to change the political culture and not just the operational political forces. Forces of moderation and stability have to mature and be given a fair opportunity to garner political clout under regimes that have reflexively and ruthlessly stifled them in the past.

Palestinians, who have been at the forefront of Arab nationalism, have generally been late in accepting and supporting the emerging Islamist movement. In addition to the overwhelming burdens of the Israeli occupation, they suffered from the generic problems of the "Arab Regime." Over the past decade, the emergence of a simple message of defiance and delivery from all ills by the slogan "Islam is the Answer" has resonated with a widening audience fed up with a corrupt and inept regime. The regime was unable to deliver on its stated goals of ending the occupation and providing freedom, security, or prosperity and has gradually lost ground to an opposition that promises a simple return to past days of glory by militancy, discipline, sacrifice, and more piety. These two forces dominated the political scene while the space between nationalist rejectionists and Islamist rejectionists has been effectively unfilled until recently.

The liberal, democratic, humanist, and secular political forces, which represent middle class interests and values, have for decades been politically marginalized, economically disadvantaged, and silenced, but not entirely vanquished. Their success and empowerment are the best guard against extremism and militancy because they have a long tradition of religious tolerance. The absence of an absolute dictatorship, together with an emerging freedom of expression, a vibrant civil society, and an educated entrepreneurial class present an opportunity for the empowerment of these forces and for a pragmatic political transformation.

A significant lesson can be drawn from the Palestinian elections of January 2005. In those elections, Mahmoud Abbas won by 62% of the vote even though his party, Fatah, represents at most only 25% of the population. Abbas campaigned on a platform based on ending the Intifada, establishing the rule of law, and conducting peaceful negotiations. It is clear that the majority of Palestinians supported his platform.

This majority of people, who have so far avoided active and organized political participation, can be retrieved, organized, and empowered in order to change Palestinian political culture. This underrepresented segment of society is ready for a liberal and democratic transformation that expands its political and economic rewards by curbing corruption and allowing the emergence of fair and free competition under the rule of law.

The Palestinians who see their future in waging a fight for freedom and independence as citizens of the global community need to be encouraged as they create a new political culture; a culture that struggles to be respectful of its own history and tradition as it adapts to life in modern times; a culture that views all other people of the world as equals as it shuns the xenophobic view of false superiority and refuses to succumb to a sense of abject inferiority; a culture that accepts the reality of globalization and its attendant political, cultural, and economic consequences; a culture that believes in the rule of law, respects the basic rights of each and every man and woman, as it demands and fights for accountability from the system and public officials.

A political vehicle that embodies this culture would be a secular, humanist, liberal, and democratic party. Its human, institutional, and material ingredients have a fragmented presence amongst the Palestinians now. Only Palestinian democrats can create such a party by pulling all its needed ingredients together. Outsiders should keep a distance and provide assistance only if requested, in order to bring this project into fruition. The ferment of this political season could provide the impetus for the birth of such a party depending on the sophistication, integrity, courage, and competence of the emerging leadership.

9. THE FUTURE OF JERUSALEM

A speech delivered by Ziad Asali, then Chairman of the Board of Directors for the American Committee on Jerusalem, to the National Council of Churches on May 30, 2001

Jerusalem confronts and challenges us all with a unique mix of the earthly and the spiritual, the secular and the religious, the mundane and the sublime. This is, of course, a mix that elicits the best from us as it invites the worst. Precisely because this city is viewed as the prize, both in a symbolic as well as a concrete sense, it drives people to want to conquer it by any means, and it is this drive, and those possible means, which make Jerusalem the most incendiary issue of our time.

There are no issues about Jerusalem that are not shrouded in controversy. To even define a moment in time in which to begin discussion of its history presents the original bias, which favors one group's claim over another's. Men of honor, as well as tendentious men with a tenuous commitment to the truth, have used all fields of human knowledge and might to buttress their group's claims to it, and to discredit the other's. It is, however, a stubborn fact that Jerusalem remains the contested home of the three monotheistic religions, and a homeland for two people, the Israelis and the Palestinians.

Three thousand years ago, David conquered the city and established the Jewish people's physical and spiritual connection to it. This connection has survived repeated destruction of temples and razing of the whole city and cycles of collective exile with their attendant sad history of ghettos, pogroms, and the Holocaust. It has remained for ages the object of their adoration and prayers.

Two thousand years ago, Jesus walked the streets of Jerusalem to preach the message of peace to the world. In this sacred city, he was crucified and ascended to Heaven, leaving the richest possible legacy of Christianity to mankind, with its non-severable links to the site of the Last Supper, Via Dolorosa, Golgotha, Calvary, and the Resurrection. Indeed, it was just over nine hundred years ago that Christian Europe marshaled its forces to reclaim Jerusalem in a Crusade that ruled it for 90 years. There is no place more central to Christianity than Jerusalem.

Fourteen hundred years ago, Prophet Muhammad preached the word of Islam, proclaiming it as a continuation of the two Abrahamic faiths. He designated Jerusalem as the first qiblah, the ordination of the five daily prayers. In Moslem tradition, it is to Jerusalem that he took his nocturnal journey, Al Isra, and from the Rock, which is housed at the Dome of the

Rock, he ascended to Heaven where he conversed with the prophets, Al Miraj. Moslems believe that the city is the site of the Day of Judgment, and the place where the angels convene.

The Arabs, under the banner of Islam, entered the city shortly after the prophet's death and established the Covenant of Omar, which guaranteed for Christians and Jews the right to live in peace in Jerusalem and to exercise religious freedom in their Holy Places. The Moslems lifted the Byzantine prohibition against the Jews in Jerusalem, thus allowing them to return. The Moslems allowed the Jews to return to Jerusalem on two more occasions, once after Saladin captured it from the Crusaders in 1187, and again when the Ottoman Sultan, Suleiman the Magnificent, opened the gates of Jerusalem to the Jews in the sixteenth century after their expulsion from Spain. Moslem and Christian Arabs have lived together in the city for the past 1500 years.

The last century witnessed momentous events in Palestine. The persecution of the Jews in Europe led to their organizing around Zionism and initiated their long process of immigration to Palestine. They were supported, with monumental effort by World Jewry, and assisted in fits and turns by various Great Powers that encoded their support in documents of immense consequence, like the Sykes-Picot agreements of 1916, the Balfour Declaration of 1917, and the UN Partition Resolution of 1947.

The establishment of the State of Israel was destined not to be peaceful. The Palestinians, who were the descendants of the residents of the land since the beginning of time, were also the titleholders to their homes, places of business, farms, and land. They fought to resist the loss of their country and property with all of their limited means. However, their resistance resulted in dual defeats. First, in 1948, Israel was established on 72% of the land of Palestine, including the west part of Jerusalem, and the refugee problem was born. Then, once again in 1967, more Palestinians were displaced when Israel completed the occupation of all of Palestine, an area that included the rest of the West Bank, including the Old City of Jerusalem, and the Gaza Strip. Israel also occupied The Sinai and the Golan Heights at that time.

Much of the conflict of the past few decades has centered on the struggle of the Palestinian people, while under occupation, to establish a state in the West Bank and Gaza with East Jerusalem as its capital. This historical compromise would have provided secure borders for Israel, a safe home for the Jewish people in the Middle East, as well as a state that the Palestinians could call their own after decades of dispossession and humiliation. However, that promise of peace, which once seemed imminent, remains elusive. Israel's practice of creating facts on the ground, with relentless settlement building, land dispossession, home demolition, and many forms of daily degradations, compounded by failure to abide by agreements, did not match its rhetoric of peace. The Palestinian Authority left itself open to charges of corruption, mismanagement, and failure to uphold principles of law or respect for human rights.

The end result was a failed peace process, confounded by dashed expectations and deepening mistrust, which led to the explosion of the Intifada. The Palestinian people could not wait for independence any longer and, when provoked, exploded in anger. The Israeli public panicked and felt besieged while their military machine subjected the whole Palestinian people to Draconian measures of siege, closure, and economic strangulation. The violence of stones and guns met with the violence of rockets, gun ships, and Apache helicopters. The dream of independence of one people clashed with the primordial fears and claims of another. The Israeli public reflexively elected a leader who offered rockets and F16's as solutions, and the region now confronts grave possibilities.

Jerusalem, as we all know, presented one of the main obstacles, if not the main obstacle, to achieving an agreement at Camp David II. It is to it that we should turn to examine our options, and probe into the possibilities of peace. Is it possible that we can fashion an agreement that accommodates the political aspirations of both the Palestinians and Israelis in Jerusalem? Is it possible that we can achieve a peace that satisfies the religious sensibilities of the Jews, Christians and Moslems? I believe we can. To argue for the exclusive merit of one group's claim, or the lack of merit of another's, is a vain attempt at avoiding serious discourse and blocking solutions. It is a prescription for disaster.

Elie Weisel, a man who won the Nobel prize for peace, someone who identifies himself as a Jew who lives in the US and not an Israeli citizen, wrote a piece in *The New York Times* on January, 24, 2001, on the topic of Jerusalem. It was a long piece, full of memory, passion, and belonging. He wrote: "Jerusalem lives within me, forever inherent in my Jewishness. It is the center of my commitments and my dreams." It is not my purpose to dissect his arguments or to cast doubt on his sincerity as he argues against the possibility of returning the Old City to the Palestinians. I will let him speak for himself as I quote "We are told that Israel's unprecedented concessions, including those on Jerusalem, were for a good cause. For peace. This is a weighty argument. Peace is the noblest of aspirations; it is worth the sacrifice of that which is most precious to us. I agree. But is it appropriate in all circumstances?

Can one always say, 'peace at any price'? To compromise on territory might seem, under certain conditions, imperative or at least politically expedient. But to compromise on history is impossible."

Mr. Weisel won his Nobel Prize for peace, but not for history. He could not compromise on history for the sake of peace. Let me tell him about history, a tiny little segment of history, that of my own family in Jerusalem. A family with a history of documented, uninterrupted presence in Jerusalem for six centuries. It is one of three notable families studied by the Israeli historian Drori Ze'evi in his book on Jerusalem in the 1600s. Mine is a family whose religious endowment, waqf, has owned properties in the Old City of Jerusalem for over two centuries. Let me tell him of the story of my own parents losing our home in Talpiot in West Jerusalem in 1948, and of our endowment, waqf, losing eleven properties cleared out to make room for a Plaza around the Wailing Wall in 1967. Let me tell him about my own living in exile with no right to return to Jerusalem because I happened to be studying abroad in 1967. Let me tell him of the Israeli military official who denied me permission to stay and practice medicine in Jerusalem thirty years ago because I did not qualify to be a resident of Jerusalem.

Let me tell Mr. Weisel that his passion for Jerusalem cannot surpass mine, that his people's passion for it provides no grounds for taking away our furnished family home. From my vantage point, his is not a tale of a beggar in Jerusalem, but rather a thief in Jerusalem, or a robber of Jerusalem. Let me tell Mr. Weisel that he cannot plead for peace for mankind, as he claims special privileges for his own kind. I am here to tell him that yes I am ready to compromise on history for the sake of peace. It is time that we all do.

I would like to tell him too that I do know about his family losses in the Holocaust, that nightmare of horror inflicted on mankind. I know and feel the sorrow of the Jews of that generation, but I am obliged to say that it was not my people's doing. Whatever redress there is for that tragedy, it should be provided. Redress for the losses and pain of my people should also be provided. The nefarious deeds that are being visited upon the Palestinians today are eating away at the prospects of such redress. A world that wants peace cannot plead ignorance of what is happening, because it has been told.

Israel has declared that it united, or reunited, Jerusalem in 1967. The joyful chorus of supporters in the American media, as well as in the US Congress, applauded this lofty concept of unity.

Let us then briefly examine the record of Israel in Jerusalem since 1967.

1. The territory of Eastern Jerusalem was extended to 73 square kilometers of Municipal Jerusalem, then to 330 square kilometers of West Bank territory of Greater Jerusalem, and then again to 660 square kilometers of West Bank territory of Metropolitan Jerusalem. This extension was designed to expand the boundaries as much as possible, and to exclude from it as many Palestinians as possible, thus providing a unique illustration of the concept of gerrymandering under occupation. Indeed, this expanded city of Jerusalem begs a single question. Which parts of the city are holy and which are simply not?

2. Israel has unilaterally declared Jerusalem as its eternal undivided capital.

3. The United Nations, the European Union, the Vatican, as well as the international community all rejected the Israeli attempt at unilateral unification.

4. The UN has gone on record with its denunciation of Israel's acts of annexation, expansion, demolition, discrimination, and unilateral changes in Jerusalem. It has demanded an end to occupation by passing more than 100 resolutions to this effect.

5. The number of Israeli settlers living on confiscated Arab land in East Jerusalem has already surpassed 200,000, thus exceeding the number of Palestinians in it.

6. The natural growth of the Palestinian population was impeded by identity card confiscation, denial of building permits, home demolitions, occupation of vacant homes, and economic strangulation as well as grossly inferior municipal services.

7. A steady emigration of Palestinian Christians from Jerusalem left a community of less than 10,000 who live in the city now, as compared with 45,000 at the time of establishment of the state of Israel. The percentage of Christians in the Holy Land has dropped from 18% to 2%. This is a grave matter that should be of utmost significance to Christians all over the world.

8. Access to Christian and Moslem holy places has been denied or restricted for the past decade to the Palestinians, as well as to all other Arabs.

9. There have been repeated military operations inside holy places, which has led, on three separate occasions, to the murder of worshippers on the grounds of the Haram al-Sharif, The Noble Sanctuary, in the past 10 years.

This record does not speak well for the status quo. Jerusalem is united now by the might of the Israeli military machine. The fact is that it continues, after 34 years of declared annexation, to be divided along ethnic, religious, cultural, and linguistic lines. This kind of coerced unity cannot be maintained. East Jerusalem is a city under occupation. There is no such thing as a moral occupation. Jerusalem must remain united but it also must be shared. The future of a Jerusalem at peace should incorporate the following three principles:

1. There can be no monopoly of sovereignty by either party. Jerusalem should be the capital of both Palestine and Israel.

2. There can be no relation of conqueror and conquered in the Jerusalem of the future. Both people should have full and equal rights to exercise all aspects of municipal governance in their respective areas.

3. No religion or nationality can be privileged in Jerusalem. The right of access to holy places and the right of worship in the city must be guaranteed for all faiths and nationalities.

These principles hold the key to a sustainable peace and any effort to subvert them, by force or guile, will serve no purpose other than to prevent a solution. It is in this context that we must say that continued land encroachment and settlement building are an act of singular irresponsibility that will preclude peace in our time. It is akin to eating the proverbial pie while negotiating to share it. It is predicated on a balance of power that is presumed will last forever. But nothing lasts forever, and memories are long. Wise people learn lessons from the Marshall Plan rather than from the Treaty of Versailles.

The principles outlined above provide guidance for evaluating the various arrangements for the people and space of Jerusalem. There is no hope for a plan that offers truncated patches of an East Jerusalem, disconnected from its own components, from its hinterland, and from the rest of Palestine. I ask you, what kind of peace do the proponents of such a plan envision? How long could it last? Have they not watched like the rest of us the fate of apartheid and bantustans?

Jerusalem has for the past decade witnessed repeated scenes of killing and bloodshed and watched the prospects for peace ebb away. It is not hard to see the logic of people resisting armed occupation by force. It is not hard to see the logic of people, who refuse to admit that they are occupiers, feeling threatened and lashing out with fury at their challengers. It is this kind of impasse that has led to the murderous cycle involving civilians.

Acts of belligerence will not come to an end without a vision of peace that is worth living for. It will not come to an end as long as one party thinks that time is on its side and that it will vanquish the other. It will not come to an end as long as one party feels that it has a monopoly on victimization, and hence, recompense. It will not come to an end as long as people of power continue to keep the fires aflame. It will not come to an end if intelligent people search for arguments to support their country right or wrong, rather than search for a reasonable compromise. It will not come to an end if good men and women stand silent in the face of injustice.

It is of justice that we speak when we speak of peace. After centuries of conflict and two world wars, Western Europe has lived in peace for the past half century, and we know it will do so for the foreseeable future because it has fashioned a foundation of justice and a vision of peace. Because we think that people of the Middle East are entitled to dream of such prospects, we should spare no effort in exploring possibilities, and offering our own vision of peace.

We think that a vision of peace for Jerusalem, based on the principles mentioned earlier, is necessary but insufficient to guide us through these difficult times. This vision, as outlined by Professor Walid Khalidi, is rooted in inclusion, not exclusion; in sharing, not monopoly; in parity, not hegemony.

It translates into the following:

1. East Jerusalem would be the capital of Palestine, with its own municipality, in the extended 1967 borders; West Jerusalem would be the capital of Israel.

2. The borders will be open and will follow the 1967 line.

3. The Jewish Quarter in the Old City, and the Wailing Wall would be under Israel sovereignty with a connecting corridor.

4. An agreed-upon number of Jewish settlements in East Jerusalem would be able to remain, and their residents would have their own boroughs. They will be Israeli citizens, with Palestinian green cards, able to vote in municipal elections.

5. The land requisitioned by Israel but not built upon would revert to the Palestinians.

6. Each religion would be in charge of its own holy places and religious institutions.

7. An inter-ministerial Jerusalem Council, with representation of both sides and with a rotating chair, would deal with political issues.

8. An inter-ecclesiastical Grand Council, with a rotating chair, would promote interfaith harmony.

9. An inter-municipal Jerusalem Council, with a rotating chair, would deal with infrastructure.

10. Palestinian former residents of West Jerusalem would have the option of compensation or return to their former properties.

11. The Jewish settlements outside the 1967 municipal borders would be subject to negotiations on settlements in the West Bank.

12. Former East Jerusalemites would be able to return to East Jerusalem.

This vision of Jerusalem of the future is fair and equitable. It provides a blueprint for a lasting peace. But will it work? Not likely, not with the present alignment of power. One can only witness what is happening in Palestine and come close to abandoning hope. How is it possible, in the days of CNN and the Internet, for a country to carry out a system of collective punishment against a whole people with the world watching on the sidelines? How much more does the individual Palestinian have to pay for being in the way, by the mere fact that he is in his/her own home?

Mr. Ariel Sharon rode to power on a wave of his people's panic, and wasted no time in issuing orders to his army, navy, and air force to blast away at civilians with rockets, as they huddled with their children in their homes. He escalated the practice of home demolition, designed to punish, to degrade, to impoverish, and to terrorize a whole family and a whole people. Can you imagine what it must feel like to have army tanks stop at your home, order you and all members of your family out instantly, and then begin to bulldoze your property, leaving you all in the street, watching the rubble of what was your home? Can you imagine this happening several times a day to families in Palestine? Can you begin to feel the pain of farmers watching bulldozers uproot acres of centuries-old olive trees and see their livelihood ruined along with their way of life? Can you comprehend what it means to the victims of such horrors to be told that Mr. Sharon will not negotiate until someone stops the violence? How about violence inflicted upon them? Do they not feel? Do they not bleed? How can Israel get away with it? It is simple. When you have your arguments so readily adopted, and actions so easily sanctioned by the Congress and the media of the only superpower in the world, you have no great need for restraint. You keep pushing until the US Secretary of State tells you that you have gone too far, using excessive and disproportionate force, and then you back off a little. So, where do we stand now?

The legal principle guiding the international effort for achieving peace remains solidly defined in the land-for-peace formulation. There is a body of international documents that has set legal boundaries for the conflict and its resolutions. These documents include UN Resolution 242, which calls for Israel's withdrawal from territories occupied in 1967, and UN Resolution 338, adopted after the 1973 war, which calls for the implementation of the previous resolutions. Then there is the Madrid Conference, whose terms of reference were based on these UN resolutions and the concept of land for peace.

The lack of implementation of the UN resolutions as they apply to Israeli withdrawal contrasts starkly with the robust and forceful implementation in other areas in the Middle East of other UN resolutions. It opens the power brokers to charges of moral inconsistency that are hard to defend. The Oslo agreements, which initiated a peace process that deferred negotiations of the crucial issues, floundered under the uneven balance of power between the two parties. After a protracted period of morbidity, it expired with the eruption of the Intifada.

In the waning days of his Presidency, Mr. Bill Clinton offered a number of proposals intended to define the parameters for an immediate settlement. These proposals dealt with four primary issues: territory, Jerusalem, refugees, and security. The Palestinians, while appreciative of his energetic involvement, felt that they could not accept his proposals because they would:

1. Divide Palestine into three separate cantons connected by Jewish only and Arab-only roads, and jeopardize the Palestinian state's viability.

2. Divide Palestinian Jerusalem into a number of unconnected islands separate from each other and the rest of Palestine.

3. Deny them the right of return.

On the issue of Jerusalem he articulated a general principle that "Arab areas are Palestinian and Jewish ones are Israeli." He also urged both sides to work to create "maximum contiguity for both." These two concepts cannot be reconciled. Israeli policy of relentless land confiscation and settlement building in and around East Jerusalem has established Jewish communities. This, along with Israel's demands for sovereignty over undefined "religious sites" outside the city wall, makes it impossible to provide for contiguity for a Palestinian Jerusalem. This formulation would result in Palestinian islands within the city separate from one another.

Mr. Clinton's proposal for the holy places provide for Palestinian sovereignty over the Haram al-Sharif and Israeli sovereignty over the Western Wall, restricting excavations beneath the Haram or behind the Wall. The Palestinians found this to be problematic because it implied that Israel has the theoretical right to excavate under the Haram. It also talked of the Western Wall rather than the Wailing Wall, thus including several hundred feet of the controversial tunnel opened by Mr. Netanyahu with bloody results in the recent past.

Mr. Clinton's proposal makes no reference to the concept of an Open City, which provides guarantees for access to holy places, and for free movement through the State of Palestine.

These proposals fell short of meeting the minimum demands for equity or international legality. By declining to accept them as presented the Palestinians were told once again that they never miss an opportunity to miss an opportunity. They, however, are holding out for the opportunity that all other people in the world have, to live in a state of their own. A state that is contiguous and undivided.

Where do we go from here?

The threat to world peace, the ghost of religious wars, is real. The local powers are hopelessly engaged in bloodletting and revenge. But this does not have to be a zero sum game. It is time—indeed it is past time—for the international community to uphold the law and implement the relevant UN resolutions. It is time for good people to make the broker more honest. It is now time to make a distinction between the occupied and the occupier, the oppressed and the oppressor, and to say enough is enough. It is now time to stand up against pressure groups that have more influence than sense. It is now time to say that peace in the world is threatened and all of us have a stake in it. We cannot stand aside fiddling while Jerusalem is burning. Men and women of good will, of all faiths and nationalities, will have to work together, in words and in deeds, to put an end to occupation, to serve the cause of justice so that we can have real peace.

10. PALESTINE AND ISRAEL: UNKIND HISTORY, UNCERTAIN FUTURE

Speech by Ziad Asali, delivered at Cornell University, September 2003

For a conflict that has been described as intractable, insoluble, and "centuries old", the most dramatic feature about the Israeli-Palestinian conflict is the near unanimous agreement about the contours of its final resolution. Think about that.

The majority of the Palestinians, Israelis, Arabs, Jews, Americans, Europeans, and people all over the world as well as global institutions are in support of an outline that goes as follows:

1. A two-state solution, Palestine alongside Israel, with borders established on international legality defined by UN Resolution 242, with minor mutually agreed-upon adjustments.

2. A shared, open Jerusalem, with the Arab part serving as a capital for Palestine and the Jewish part serving as the capital of Israel.

3. End of occupation and settlements.

4. A fair and equitable solution of the refugee problem, based on international legality, with resettlements, compensation, and redress of moral and psychological grievances.

5. End of conflict and a complete cessation of violence between Israel and all Arab states, including Palestine, with open borders and normalized relations for all.

6. A Marshall Plan to rebuild Palestine and provide an underpinning for a lasting peace.

The Alternatives

The alternatives to this solution, one secular state, a bi-national state, continued occupation and apartheid, or mass transfer of millions of Palestinians, are not worthy of serious discussion at this point in our history, although they are bandied about. Jews did not struggle to be free of gentile domination and to have a state of their own only to end up negotiating giving it up to live in a secular state. A bi-national state requires a minimum of cooperation and coordination between equal partners, an option that we do not have at this point in time. Transferring millions of people is a political and physical fantasy that cannot be realized. There is no possible reason to expect that the Palestinian people will give up their national project for independence. They will never accept to live under apartheid nor settle for a rump, truncated, or dependent state. All these options are but varying recipes for continued strife.

If the question is when do we achieve the solution rather than what kind of a solution are we to expect, it is supremely frustrating to witness the unending murders, the injuries, the demolitions and the sheer destruction, and fear the people of both sides must endure before sanity prevails and peace is restored. It is hard to imagine in these days of turmoil, but it is indeed possible, that both people can live, build, enjoy, and contribute to humankind.

Palestinian parents should not live in fear that their children will be killed by an Israeli soldier or a missile while walking on the way to school just as Israeli parents should not live in fear that their children will be blown up by a suicide bomber on the bus that takes them to school.

Why is it, we ask, do we have such a congruity of spoken objectives and paucity of implementation? Why is the will of dedicated extremist minorities in each society able to frustrate the will of the majorities and exercise its veto power with spectacular acts of violence against innocent civilians on both sides? Why are we, here in this hall, like so many hundreds of millions across the globe, concerning ourselves so seriously with a conflict that is thousands of miles away in a small piece of land?

There are no easy answers but there are ways to explore and probe, and it is my intention to do just that today.

A Brief Synopsis

Let me start out by presenting the briefest possible synopsis of the history of this modern conflict: Jewish people, persecuted in Europe, and denied elementary justice came to the conclusion that they had to band together and establish a Jewish state free from gentile oppression. They started to immigrate to Palestine around the end of the 19th century, secured a legal foundation for their homeland from the British in 1917, and from the United Nations in 1947. Israel was established on 78% of the land of Palestine in 1948 and hundreds of thousands of Palestinians left and became refugees. In 1967, the rest of Palestine, known as the West Bank and Gaza, was captured by Israel in the Six-Day War and has remained under occupation ever since. Around three and a half million Palestinians live under occupation as we speak. This, ladies and gentleman, is the longest lasting occupation of modern times and the quest of the Palestinians for their freedom from this occupation and for establishing their own state is at the core of this conflict.

The problem with history is that it has been around for too long. It has provided arguments, based in fact, fiction, or perceived wisdom, for each party to the conflict and even to those who seem to have no axe to grind.

The Two Narratives

There are two basic irreconcilable narratives that draw sustenance from history: In the most simplistic terms, the Jewish Zionist narrative, driven by memory of the Holocaust, claims the Holy Land as the Promised Land which is the patrimony of the Jews ordained by God and no one else has the right to it. Expansion, settlement building, expropriation of Palestinian lands, and appropriation of their water resources are natural consequences to this ideology. Security considerations evoked to demolish homes, transfer people or punish cities and towns with curfews, closures, impoverishment, and humiliation find a receptive audience in subscribers to this narrative. Extremists in the settler movement and fanatics in political or military circles want to hold on to the dream of Eretz Israel free of Palestinians. They think they can militarily defeat the Palestinians and extinguish the idea of Palestine in Arab minds. They have no patience for those who voice concerns and raise issues of Palestinian national rights, demographics, or basic human rights.

The Palestinian narrative, again in its crudest and most elementary form, is that of their dispossession by an alien, more powerful force with a bogus religious claim to the land. It is a tale of suffering from continued land-grab, dispossession, disinheritance, displacement coupled with powerlessness and with the virtual absence of an organized and effective military. It is oblivious to the suffering of the Jews in Europe and to the Holocaust and innocent of any knowledge of pogroms or ghettos. All it feels is its own victimization and illegal usurpation of what it once had. A sense of justice violated and dignity insulted infuses and sustains its psychology of resistance. This mix has led to, and will continue to feed, a violent and bizarre phenomenon that has defined the Palestinians like no other people: the phenomenon of suicide bombing and political murder of civilians. Extremists, be they secular or religious, have refused to accept the Israel of 1948 or 1967, and hope to liberate the land from Zionism. They view the two-state solution as a compromise of the weak and have used all means to frustrate a political compromise.

Fear and Loathing

These two narratives have come into clash, and have bred a political establishment, whether religious or secular, in either society, that contributed to a sense of **monopoly on victimization**. Steeped in fear, anger, and frustration, a significant minority of each population has little room for acknowledging, let alone feeling, the pain of the other. Even more starkly, one can say that each segment views the suffering of the other as just revenge and deserved punishment. Compromise sounds to such people like appeasement and weakness, if not outright treason. With every act of murderous violence inflicted on civilians people in each society become increasingly receptive to the racist, fascist arguments, sometimes openly stated but more often felt and implied, "They are not human; they understand nothing but force and violence; we should never show them any mercy because they will think it is a sign of weakness; a face for an eye and time is on our side."

However, there is a growing sense of battle fatigue; devastated lives and economies, a sense of fear and despair of a better future for the children: the Palestinians fear that they may never have a state, and some Israelis fear that the future of Israel itself is in doubt. There is genuine concern on both sides for the corrupting and decaying influence of the conflict on both societies and their values.

If history has taught us anything, it has taught us this: **Left to their own devices the Palestinians and Israeli will simply not be able to resolve this conflict. Period.**

The gross imbalance of power between the parties, the erosion of the political clout of the peace camp in both sides, the depth of hostility that breeds a phenomenon like suicide bombing, and the hardening of Israeli attitudes manifested by tolerance of missiles directed at urban centers, are but a few factors that support such a conclusion. Were it a viable option, the rest of the world, as well as some American administrations including this one, might wish to take a Rhett Butler approach, to walk away and frankly not give a damn. All serious people, however, realize that this not possible.

The Story of Our Times

The Israeli-Palestinian conflict is the central story of our times; it encapsulates in a tiny patch of land, with a small number of people, the sum total of large human conflicts throughout history. An incendiary mix of religions, cultures, civilizations, races, and ethnic groups has provided the historical setting for the clashes of modern times: liberation versus oppression; freedom versus occupation; self-determination versus colonialism; fanaticism versus secularism; traditionalism versus modernism; capitalism versus a mix of defunct socialism or feudalism; justice versus power; chaos versus complexity; corruption versus idealism; the third world versus the white man and his proxy; and F-16s versus the suicide bomber. Indeed, there are many more elements of drama within and among these societies that do not allow this conflict to be neatly contained and confined to the combatants. At the least numerical assignation, it will pit 1.2 billion Muslims worldwide against the West.

Of all the political and social ills that afflict the Arab and Muslim people, the Palestine story has captured their imagination and touched their core feelings of violation and powerlessness. This is the stuff that breeds terror. A metaphysical, absolutist, cold cadre of operatives seeking self-annihilation is roaming the land. A self-replicating enemy that is driven by issues put to deadly use. An enemy that you can defeat not by annihilation, but by denying it the opportunity to exploit issues that burn in the hearts of young people yearning to fight injustice.

Fear, anger, despair, injustice, and an almost exclusive sense of victimization on both sides have their most damaging consequences in narrowing the space needed for policy options. Public discourse is stunted, simplistic, and crude. Sloganeering has taken the place of honest analysis in many political and media circles. It is easier in this climate to follow the safe course of demonizing and dehumanizing the "other." To assume the worst and to impugn the motives of the other is much safer than to explore possibilities of compromise and working out solutions, wherein you run the risk of being labeled as naïve at best, and a sell out at worst. Politicians, even the few with courage, are caught in this logic and find it more prudent to assign all blame to the declared enemies on the other side than to forthrightly address their own constituents. The tried and true policies of the past, built on total mistrust with aggressive intent, are much more convenient to pursue and will bring about yet more catastrophes and mayhem. These fundamentally violent policies have born this rotten fruit. Their logic, which traps traditional decision makers on either side, makes it imperative to have a third party intervene and take charge to lead us all out of this deadly impasse.

United States National Interest

Make no mistake: We in this country have a fundamental national security interest in addressing and resolving, rather than merely "managing," the Israeli-Palestinian conflict. **No single decision we make can top the resolution of this conflict to enhance our national security.** We also happen to be the only party in the world that is capable of doing so. We have the leverage with billons of dollars doled out to Israel annually, and a hundred million dollars given to the Palestinians annually. We have the political, military, and social tools needed to make our choices and proposed solutions carry the weight we want. We have media with the global reach to add credibility to the policies that we may chose to adopt. Our longstanding, tried, and tested commitment to the existence and well-being of Israel should give it enough assurance that we will stand by our commitment and see it through. The Palestinians have but one party left in the world that can deliver to them a State of Palestine and that is us.

The fact is that we are the one indispensable party to the solution. We have historically leaned heavily towards Israel. It has been an emotional issue, a domestic policy issue. We have managed to steer it in such a way that it has not adversely affected our relations with the Arab and Muslim governments but certainly not with their people. The seething anger of the Arab and Muslim people had not manifested itself to us prior to 9/11 and the power of incitement of Arab satellite TV stations had not channeled the anger of the masses against us so visibly before. The Palestinian issue has not motivated Bin Laden and Al Qaeda but it is the key to diffusing and containing their influence. It is in our interest as Americans to do so. Dealing seriously with this issue is not, as some claim, caving in to terrorism; on the contrary, it is precisely the best tool to defeat it.

Our choice to support a State of Palestine alongside Israel, as voiced by the President on many occasions, should be the beginning of establishing a genuine democratic, constitutional state, with modern tools of governance, transparency, free speech, free enterprise, and free men and women protected by law. This, more than any other decision, will help steer that region away from the scourge of terrorism and fanatical religious extremism. The US itself has lacked credibility in its failure to be an honest broker in the past; Tenet, Mitchell, Zini, and now the Roadmap are proposals and agreements that were crying out for implementation. None of them is perfect, however, it is now our challenge to implement what we proposed, adopted, and celebrated: the plan of the day is the Roadmap, which both the Palestinians and the Israelis have accepted.

We, like all enablers, have let violations of this agreement go unpublicized, unchecked and unpunished. We have condemned terrorism with every breath we exhale and asked the Palestinian Authority to "do more" to eradicate it. All successive Israeli prime ministers have been unable to root out terrorism, including Sharon who placed no limits on his army as they dealt out collective punishment to the whole Palestinian society. No Palestinian Authority can accomplish this task outside a political framework. Addressing this conflict exclusively as a security problem without resolving the political issues simultaneously has been a miserable policy failure. It is, in fact, a recipe for extending the period of suffering and mayhem.

What is to be done?

It is time that we think more of our children's future than our father's past. Should we decide to measure up to the task of resolving this conflict in our time we have the following steps to ponder:

1. We need to agree clearly on objectives such as the proposed historic compromise of a two-state solution based UN Resolution 242. Confidence building measures that are supposed to lead us to an "end game" are doomed because the parties involved have consistently failed to demonstrate any measure of good will that justifies confidence.

2. We need to establish bridges among people and institutions that support the historic compromise of all religions, ethnicities, and backgrounds. Such bridges need to develop into political mechanisms and tools to impact decision making.

3. We need to isolate extremists, secular and fundamentalists, and to expose their threat to peace and to universal values of equality of people. Each group has a special obligation to speak out against extremists within its own ranks and to condemn their actions.

4. The US can begin to seriously resolve this conflict only if it has the political will to do so. Its credibility will be measured by the public and effective measures taken to:

    a. Support a two-state solution based on UN Resolution 242.

    b. Lead the parties to implement the existing agreements and bring to a halt any and all measures, including the wall/fence, that preclude the compromise.

    c. Provide for and oversee a program for security in the West Bank and Gaza under American supervision. Security will never be provided by any of the local combatants and it has to be a third-party domain.

    d. Oversee an international economic aid package to rebuild the country and secure the peace.

5. Palestinian leaders, in and out of office, should promulgate and generate support for a document about their own vision of the "final status." Clear positions need to be articulated about the controversial issues like Jerusalem, refugees, and borders. All acts of violence against civilians should be condemned and must cease. Honest communication

with the people about the needed compromises cannot be avoided much longer. This process should lead to debate, reform, and elections.

6. Arab leaders must also share the collective responsibility for compromise and those who shirk this responsibility must face political consequences. They should engage their public and the world in support of the Beirut Arab League resolution to end the conflict.

7. Israeli supporters of the historic compromise, in and out of office, should organize and state their position in public. Renunciations of metaphysical claims that justify land grab are fundamental to the package that leads to the end of conflict with no further claims. Occupying other people's land and lording it over them cannot be sustained. Incremental land grab that precludes the formation of a viable Palestinian state must cease. Violence against civilians must cease. Jewish people in Israel and all over the world must hold those who perpetrate the measures taken in their name into account.

8. We, all of us, need to push in every way we can for expanding the scope of freedom in the Arab and Islamic World. This cannot be done by forcing a grotesque emulation of Western democracies, but rather by a steady program of opening up and securing economic opportunities, educational reform, and accountable governments. The West can genuinely help rather than pontificate and condescend. The Palestinian issue should be removed as an excuse or justification for all the actions that Arab governments undertake.

9. American and international institutions and individuals should organize a superfund to support the private sector and provide humanitarian aid to rebuild the Palestinian society.

The measures just outlined can lead to resolution of this conflict.

This is not a good versus evil saga. It is rather a sad tale of two peoples caught in a web of debris from an unkind history.

Nothing we do, however, can substitute for a serious understanding of the issues, one that keeps our grasp on universal human values intact as we labor in our quest to do the best we can. This issue has become too serious to be left to politicians alone. When future historians write about our era, they will either ask what went wrong or how catastrophe was avoided. It is up to us, all of us, to provide them with an answer.

11. ON THE HISTORIC COMPROMISE

Speech by Ziad Asali, delivered at Cornell University, November 4, 2004

A confluence of factors makes this historical moment of singular uncertainty. One of these is the political turmoil in Israel over the Gaza Disengagement Plan, which has not been resolved by the vote in Knesset in its favor, and the other is the acute deterioration of the health of Yasser Arafat, and his departure from Palestine, with seismic implications for Palestinian policy and politics. All prognostications at this time are fraught with danger, and are better called guesswork. I will take a stab at this later on in my speech.

Pervez Musharraf, the President of Pakistan, was asked by Peter Jennings in a televised interview on the evening news on September, 20, 2004, if he thought that the US could lose the war on terror. Musharraf answered, "Well, if you don't go addressing political disputes, yes. That is a possibility." When pressed as to what he thought the principal political dispute that must be addressed was, Musharraf's answer was, "First of all, Palestine. Because I think that has the maximum negative perspective all around the Muslim world, whether they are concerned or not. There is unanimous sympathy for the Palestinians against the Israelis. And the US is seen or perceived as an Israeli supporter and totally against Muslims. So I think this is the one which needs to be resolved immediately."

Now, President Musharraf is arguably one of America's most, if not the most, important allies in the war against terror, a man who has survived several assassination attempts and plots, who lives in the Bin Laden neighborhood of Afghanistan and Waziristan, is the leader burdened with dealing with the intractable problem of Kashmir that pits his country against a nuclear adversary in India, and is at the vortex of the fight against poverty, fanaticism, and terror in his own country. He is a survivor and a seasoned leader who earned the respect of friend and foe. His capital, Karachi, is separated from Jerusalem by five countries and nearly two thousand miles. For this man to unhesitatingly name the Palestinian conflict as the primary dispute that needs to be resolved immediately is a most telling statement.

The most significant weapons in the hands of terrorists are the issues they use to recruit and behind which they take cover. The Palestine question could not be more appealing for the terror masters to appropriate. It touches the core forces that shape all of us before we develop the ability to reason and reflect—forces like our history, faith, race, ethnicity, civilization, culture, country, and geography. Add to this the incendiary mix of a sense of victimization, economic deprivation, land expropriation, images of death, destruction, and humiliation flashing daily on satellite TV screens and you can get a sense of the value of this issue to adopt and to mobilize.

The majority of world powers, as well as majority of the people surveyed globally, have arrived at an international consensus, which has been defined but not implemented, and is known as the 'Historic Compromise.' It is outlined in President Clinton's letter to the parties in the waning days of his presidency in 2001. This compromise is summed up as follows:

- Two states, living side by side, in peace with an end to the conflict.

- Borders are based on those before 1967, with mutually agreed upon modifications.

- A shared Jerusalem, with Arab East Jerusalem as the capital of Palestine, and Jewish Jerusalem as capital of Israel.

- A solution for the 1948 refugee problem that redresses their grievances without compromising the characters of both states based on international legality. These include compensation, mutually agreed upon repatriation and relocation, as well as an acknowledgement of the rights the Palestinians have for losses sustained in the catastrophe that befell them in 1948.

- End of occupation and evacuation of settlements.

- A Marshall Plan to build the foundations of Palestine and the foundations of peace.

This formulation preserves the core needs of both people. Israel will have a state with secure and defined borders at peace and the Palestinians will have their own secure and guaranteed state serving as a home for all Palestinians who wish to live in it.

The price for the Israelis in this compromise is to give up on the concept of Eretz Israel, or Greater Israel, with its expansive territorial ambitions and to withdraw from the Occupied Territories. For the Palestinians, the price is to accept the loss of 78% of their land by abandoning claims of the areas defined by the establishment of the State of Israel in 1948. Claims to the whole land, mostly articulated with passion by religious advocates based on interpretations of Holy Texts on all sides, are a recipe for an endless bloody conflict and have to be disowned by the majority of both peoples. This is the crux of the substance of peace.

The will of the majority, expressed in this compromise, has been thwarted by that of a minority on both sides. The minority on either side has had the political clout, and has not hesitated to act decisively, to derail all political initiatives for peace.

Violence, mostly against civilians, has been used by these forces as an effective veto, as well as an educational tool, about the futility of compromise. Hardening of the position of the public, and weakening of the peace camp on both sides are direct results of the calculated use of violence that diminishes hope. There is a paradoxical congruity of purposes of people opposed to a compromise—both sides think that time is on their side. The Israeli opposition thinks that if they hang tough and hold on to the West Bank, the Palestinians will give up and the world will forget about them and move on. The Palestinian opposition thinks of Israel as a Crusader outpost that will in time, perhaps a century or two, meet the fate of the last Crusade of a thousand years ago, at the hands of an Islamic power. In short, both views write the same prescription for a bloody century.

This conflict has generated the longest lasting occupation in modern times. The role that ethnic and religious zealots on all sides have played in its continuation is a testament to the power of mixing religion with politics. This power, if it goes unchecked and unconfronted by the Rule of Law and reason, can be as destructive as all weapons known to man.

The US, as the only standing superpower, with its established constitutional and historical tradition of the rule of law, and the separation of Church and State, is uniquely qualified to act as an intermediary in bringing this conflict to a close. It is, however, not merely a neutral and disinterested party that is called upon to lend its good offices for the task. It is a country with global interests, with its own moral and economic imperatives and with a dynamic and contested political system that yields to pressures and counter pressures. It is fair to say, that all these ingredients have been at play in shaping the US policy on the Palestinian-Israeli conflict. The role of the honest broker, articulated for sometime, has yielded to that of a patron and protector of Israel. The creation of a Palestinian state, and all the attendant benefits that may accrue to the Palestinians, are predicated on the security and assured existence of Israel with its unique mix of a Jewish and democratic character as defined by Israel. It is clear that the historic compromise, outlined earlier, does provide for this stipulation. The questions that need to be answered now are: Are the parties themselves capable of working out the mechanisms of the desired deal? Is the US convinced of the need for a lasting peace? And lastly, is it willing and able to exert itself to bring the whole conflict to an end?

The Israelis and Palestinians have been involved in a poisonous feud, with an escalating thirst for revenge fueled by blood and sorrow, inflicted by emboldened extremists in ascendance on both sides.

The Palestinian body politic, on the one hand, has been dysfunctional. It is fragmented and plagued by erosion of hope and encroaching lawlessness. Occupation, with its severe and destructive measures that adopted collective humiliation as a policy, has delivered withering blows to the Palestinian society and its institutions. Incompetence, coupled with corruption, loss of control over violence, and the rise of lawlessness and extremism, have all contributed to the loss of moral authority of its historic leadership. These factors combined can make it very difficult to negotiate and deliver an acceptable compromise. Recent developments, with possible changes in leadership, may present an opportunity, but that, by itself, is insufficient.

The Israelis, on the other hand, have witnessed an emerging and widening clout of extremist, xenophobic, and militant forces coalescing around the settler movement and committed to thwart compromise. The murder of Prime Minister Rabin for his serious commitment to a compromise led eventually to the ascendance of Mr. Sharon, one of the most militant Israeli prime ministers and a historic opponent of compromise. The passionate resistance to Sharon's disengagement plan from Gaza, with loud public calls for his murder, is an indication of the difficulties that Israel faces in making the serious compromises needed for peace. Significant political realignments, which may very well be under way, are needed for Israel to be ready for the kind of negotiations required for attaining peace.

The recent trends, in both sides may open up the door for serious political developments. However, it is reasonable to conclude, that these two parties, left to their own devices, will not be able to achieve peace. This conflict has become more central, less comfortable to talk about, and more defined in terms of the disparity of power between the occupied and occupier since September 11. Paradoxically, there is a genuine fear in Israel and in the US for the long-term security of Israel precisely at the time that Israel has achieved military superiority over all the combined forces of the Arab States. The sources for the perceived long-term threat are Islamic powers motivated by the newly infused call for Jihad unleashed by the Iranian Revolution and by the ingathering of Islamic militants in Afghanistan who fought successfully against the Soviet Union. The goal of the new Islamist militant movement is to unite over a billion people under the banner of Islam and to confront the West and its surrogates.

Understanding this threat, without designating an order of probability to it, makes it more urgent for Israel to resolve the core issue between it and the Palestinians bilaterally. The Palestinians, chafing under the longest occupation in modern times, weakened and bloodied, can and would settle for a viable state to end this conflict, and with it, their claim to the land they lost in 1948. Israel, at the height of its military power, and perhaps at the beginning of a political decline in its international standing, has clear incentives to make such a deal with the Palestinians in order to avoid a century of confrontation with over a billion Muslims. The Arabs, and Muslims, can hardly have a claim to settle if the Palestinians accept a final peace settlement.

It is not a forgone conclusion that the US is indeed convinced of the need and urgency of resolving this issue. Several presidents have stated their support for the general outline of the compromise, and most recently, President Bush came out publicly in support of a Palestinian state. However, the argument has not been made, nor politically endorsed by any administration, for the great need to resolve this issue because of our own national interest. The rising wave of global terror that erupted dramatically on September 11, originating from the Arab and Muslim world, should indeed be confronted by force and without compromise. However, to leave its causes and consequences unexamined is political malpractice. It is quite unlikely that Bin Laden had Palestine in mind when he launched his attack. However, he has latched on to it since then, and we have seen evidence of that in his most recent TV appearance during this campaign. He fully understands the resonance of this theme with the masses. President Musharraf, arguably the staunchest and the most exposed ally in this global fight against terror, understands this too. He is willing, courageously, to state his position to a worldwide audience. Depriving the bin Ladens of this world of this issue will deny them their single most effective tool for recruitment and support. There is little doubt that terrorists will persist for a long time after the Palestine question is laid to rest. However, they could no longer count on the support of angry people frustrated by our policy on Palestine. Resolving it is necessary but insufficient in our quest for stability and peace. The global atmospherics and discourse will be dramatically ameliorated. Leaders will be able to make the needed compromises without fear of punishment for "selling out". It is for this reason, above all, that we need to commit our energy and resources to act to resolve it.

Terror, amongst other things, is a tool by ruthless leadership to manipulate the poor, the weak, and the disenfranchised in order to change the status quo. Alleviating poverty and giving a structure and hope to the lives of the people by effective economic measures, will detract from the appeal of its advocates. The Palestinian-Israeli conflict has been a stumbling block on the road to developing normal trade relations between the 1.2 billion Muslims, three hundred million of whom are Arabs, and the West, especially the US. Normalizing trade relations is a prerequisite for development if done with proper safeguards. Pursuing a serious policy aiming towards improving the life conditions of the people of these countries is an essential safeguard against the nihilistic and destructive tools of terror. The goal should be to create employment opportunities and strengthen the purchasing power of the people rather than their leadership. The prospect of opening up new and vast markets for our goods and products should not escape the attention of our business people.

The commitment to spread freedom, foster democracy, and advocate values of individual and societal fulfillment and prosperity, is appropriately articulated. This commitment, made because of our own self-interest, has to be credible and to be perceived as such. The short cuts of the past have led us to the present. It is in this context again that a genuine policy to build a constitutional, democratic, accountable state in Palestine, committed to building institutions based on the rule of law, will bear most fruit. The Palestinian society is not encumbered by a history of a state and its intrusive might. Civil society is vibrant and critical, with more active NGOs than most neighboring states. The public is clamoring for elections and participation. Indeed, the events of the past week or two make these elections suddenly attractive, practical, and the best legitimizing tool for the new leadership. The Palestinians are some of the most educated people in the Middle East, with a Diaspora that lead them to all four corners of the world, where they learned, participated, and prospered. As a result, they are especially qualified to build a vibrant democracy. Nothing is more consistent with our values of freedom and rule of law than assisting the Palestinians to build their own system based on these principles.

Considering the significance of the resolution of this conflict, and the fact that it enjoys the support of the Quartet, the Arab League, the majority of the Palestinians and Israelis as well as their governments, let alone the support of 70% of Americans, American Jews, and Arab Americans, it is nothing short of astonishing that it was not even featured as a topic worthy of discussion in the Presidential foreign policy debate. It has hardly received any attention in the national Presidential campaign. In a significant policy statement, President Bush reiterated in April of this year his support of a two-state solution as he reaffirmed the US steadfast support for Israel's security. He also called for a new Palestinian leadership not compromised by terror. He committed the US to support the establishment of a Palestinian state that is viable, contiguous, sovereign, and independent. He welcomed the disengagement from Gaza and some settlements in the West Bank as real progress and as a bold initiative. He added that it would be unrealistic to expect a full withdrawal to the 1949 armistice line. This takes into account the demographics and the new population centers, otherwise known as facts on the ground. He accepted the barrier as a security, and not a political border, and stated that it should be temporary rather than permanent.

During this campaign, Senator Kerry endorsed and supported all these new positions adopted by President Bush in his April 14, 2004 speech. He made it a point to restate his personal, emotional, and deep commitment to Israel. He gave the following promise to the people of Israel:

- We will never pressure you to compromise your security.

- We will never expect you to negotiate for peace without a credible partner.

- We will always work to provide the political and military and economic help for your fight against terror.

The national debate about this issue could not been have been more superficial nor less substantive. It is summed up by a common strategy of heaping calumny on the Palestinian leadership and declaring Arafat an unacceptable partner for negotiations, which practically meant no negotiation with any Palestinian. Palestinian terror had to cease before negotiations, which again meant no negotiations. No criticism was directed against Israel's harsh occupation policy, or against building the wall/fence on Palestinian land, or its unceasing building of settlements. The commitment to Israel's security was stated on every occasion the subject came up, which is not often, and the Palestinian security was never mentioned. Palestinian civilian casualties—"collateral damage"— inflicted by the Israeli army were always seen as retaliation against terror. All in all, a packaged program meant to avoid criticism by anyone who remotely identifies with the Israeli government. Most of the Jewish and Zionist organizations found little to criticize in either candidate's policy testimonials. Some leaders of the emerging fundamentalist Christians thundered their divine wrath against the very possibility of compromise and wise heads nodded in profound acquiescence.

Now that the silly season is behind us, what can we look for? Much will depend on where the Palestinian question will fit in the strategy of the US in the war on terror in general, the war on Iraq, and the perception of the President and his team of its centrality in reshaping and remolding the Middle East of the future. The new political realities in Palestine will make it possible to engage in serious negotiations, and may indeed provide the counterpart to the forces in Israel that is serious about peace. The US may find the new political realities easier to reconcile with the national interest.

Much will depend on the definition of the national interest. If it is defined by a security-minded, global war against terrorism, with Palestinian acts of violence falling squarely under this rubric, it is likely that we will see a green light to Israel to pursue a military solution postponing, or more flamboyantly embalming, the whole project of the Palestinian state and all the vexing final status issues associated with it. The Gaza Disengagement plan will be the only plan in play for years to come and all the political discourse and jockeying will center on its implementation and its implications. The future of the West Bank and Jerusalem will be left in doubt to be determined by the ever-changing facts on the ground. The new Palestinian leadership will be allowed to play a role confined to Gaza and some northern parts of the West Bank with an indefinite conversation about the rest.

A more benign, compassionate if you will, definition of the national interest, will have to be more comprehensive than this and will address the political, economic, and cultural dimensions of the Middle East policy. This definition will lead to the creation of a viable Palestine by identifying and empowering legitimate Palestinian leadership, and it means working with the Israelis to create this state. Committing to this goal publicly, the US and Israel will have little difficulty finding the right partners. A long, drawn out period of implementation, needed to maximize security and to generate attitudinal, economic, and political changes, will be tolerated if the end game is clearly stated at the outset with early visible and concrete steps taken. Empowering the new Palestinian leadership, in concrete terms by concrete measures, reflected on the daily life of the Palestinian people, is the single most significant step towards peace and stability.

Resolving the Israeli-Palestinian conflict will need the personal commitment of the President, which would be best expressed by his appointing an envoy empowered to see this project through. The person selected will have to have solid credentials and will need to enjoy the full confidence of the President. President Bush, elected with a 3.5 million vote margin of victory, with a Republican majority in the House and Senate, has the mandate and power to implement his policy. He will be able to make his policy choices based on his vision of the national interest without political considerations.

National interest is not an objective scientific reality. It is based on choices made by the political leaders who are the winners of the multitude of contending and competing forces in the nation. The Israeli-Palestinian conflict in this country has reflected the influence of a coalition of forces that cuts across many segments of the nation in support of Israel. This coalition had deep roots in the Democratic Party as well as serious support in the Republican Party, the business community as well as Labor unions, the defense establishment as well as white and black liberals, fundamentalist Christians as well as Jews, the media, and academia.

It is possible, in theory, to think of a coalition of forces that share a common interest in a two-state solution. Those who want a safe and secure Israel as well as those who want to create a peaceful and secure Palestine share this goal above all. These strange bedfellows should be at the core of this alliance. People who are interested in peace, in stemming the tide of extremism and militant religious fundamentalists of every stripe, human rights groups who see the prospect of a constitutional and democratic Palestine as template for the Arab world, corporations and business people who stand to make profit in a stabilized Middle and Near East, the progressive wing of the Democratic party and the moderate wing of the Republican party, the civil rights community, various ethnic communities, as well as the academic and intellectual community, the C-Span crowd—that has an understanding of the implications of policy and strategy—all these groups are potential allies in this single-issue coalition that has yet to emerge. No link has tied these groups together as of yet.

The academic and intellectual community, arguably the societal equivalent of the central nervous system, has the unique ability to germinate the ideas and motivate the youth to guide this movement. The budding confrontation and polarization on campuses, generally driven by idealism and a quest for justice, with a large dose of tribalism and passion, should be channeled into a serious movement to achieve a defined achievable objective rather than to score debating points. In so doing it can make a singular contribution to world peace. What is needed on campuses is an alliance for a two-state solution. At the core of this alliance, or coalition, should be Palestinian, Israeli, Arab, Muslim, and all American members of the academic community who are serious about peace. It is hard to ask members of the academic community to engage less in scoring debating points, and more in the hard work of building a genuine political coalition and working to impact policy, but it is important.

This coalition can be built around a single issue, the 'Historic Compromise.' Talk of a bi-national, or one state, à la South Africa, is yet one more model for non-peace. The Jewish people of Israel, who have dreamt for millennia of their state and fought for it, will not peacefully surrender it after losing a debate. The Palestinians who have suffered exile, occupation, and second-class citizenship for two generations should settle for nothing less than a viable and free state of their own. The future relations of these two states should be left to future generations. To call for a bi-national state now is to resign us to decades of conflict and this choice has to be understood by all. It is a choice and not a destiny. The energy of young men and women can best be spent to define the elements of the 'Historic Compromise,' to carve out a better future for these two peoples, rather than to dwell on the pain of the present and the past, and by doing so to perpetuate it.

It is hard in the passions of the moment, with so much suffering and pain, to speak of a dispassionate compromise. There are, however, new political realities in Israel and in Palestine that make this issue less likely to ignore, and, more optimistically, less intractable to tackle. The presence in the White House, of a decisive leader, with a strong mandate can provide the indispensable ingredient of the arbiter of peace.

In Israel, the disengagement plan has pitted the super-hawk and father of the settlements, Sharon, against the settlers and their supporters in his own party. It has made it necessary for Sharon to seek an alliance with the Labor and other peace groups and to confront his own religious extremist past supporters. Regardless of his intentions, that are suspect by the majority of the Palestinians who see this as a ploy to hold on to the West Bank, he is creating a serious challenge to the metaphysical hold on the land. This will have ramifications for the future.

The Palestinian President Yasser Arafat, the only leader they have known for the past four decades has fallen ill and has been moved to Paris. The long and deep shadow that he cast on Palestinian, and regional, politics will be cast over politicians of lesser stature, if not more skill. The challenge for the Palestinians and their leaders is to hold the supremacy of their established institutions and to effectuate a political transition under occupation without violence or civil strife: A most challenging feat.

These new political realities offer a unique mix of variables that can be utilized to bring about compromise, negotiations and peace. They just as plausibly could lead to chaos, and worse, persistent conflict with global ramifications. Decisions made by our newly elected president, with the prodding political support of an engaged and committed coalition for compromise, can translate the promise of the moment to a reality of peace. It is left to us, to our country, the only superpower left standing, and to our people, to pursue this promise for the sake of global peace, and because it is in our interest, and also, because it is the right thing to do.

12. THE WAY FORWARD IN THE MIDDLE EAST PEACE PROCESS
House Committee on International Relations

Submitted for the record by Ziad Asali, MD
President, American Task Force on Palestine

Chairman Hyde, distinguished members of the Committee:

Thank you for giving me the privilege to be here today to discuss with you the future of peace in the Middle East.

The American Task Force on Palestine was founded to promote the view that creating a state of Palestine, living alongside Israel in peace, is vital to the national security of our country. We are gratified by the diplomatic progress that has taken place this week.

Last month, it was my honor to be a member of the official delegation our government sent to observe the Palestinian elections. The group was comprised of eight members: Senators Biden and Sununu, two Palestinian Americans—I being one of them—and four senior senatorial staff members who were later joined by the US Consul General in Jerusalem. In an intense and compact program we met with the two Palestinian front runners and, separately, with the Palestinian and Israeli Prime Ministers, the leaders of the International Observers, President Carter, and Prime Ministers Rocard of France and Bilt of Sweden. We also met with the President of the Palestinian Election Committee and his senior staff.

To me, and perhaps to others, by far the most fascinating and energizing part of this trip was the contact with the Palestinian people. We visited eight voting stations. Three of these were in Ramallah and Al-Bireh, four in

Jerusalem—at Jaffa Gate, Shufat, Al-Tor, Mount Scopus, and Salaheddin Street—and finally, at closing time, we visited Bethany Al Ayzariyyeh to observe the closing of the vote and counting of ballots. These places were the stomping grounds of my youth. No experience in my life can match the singular mix of emotions that I felt that day. A host of passions swelled within me, a sense of pride and humility, of strength and vulnerability, hope and trepidation, a sense of identity and identification as I moved around people familiar and not so familiar. Here I was, a member of my country's delegation to my home town, the place of my birth and the home of my forefathers, come to bear witness to the birth of democracy, and to the promise of an independent state. I felt the overwhelming sense of being part of a significant piece of history in the making.

I went around asking many questions: "How do you feel? Has anybody intimidated you? Bribed you? Tried to dissuade you from voting? Or to prevent you from traveling?" The answer was uniform and consistent: "No, no one did." After getting over their early suspicions, many of them were eager to talk. The 85 year-old grandmother assisted by two of her grandchildren told me, "This is my right." The middle aged professional woman said, "We did not need a campaign. We know what we are doing, and we know whom to vote for." And there were the young men insisting on visiting all stations in Jerusalem until they found the one with their names listed. The children were playful and at one point, broke out around us in a chant about the elections. Pictures were taken. Adults were somber. They did not know what to make of me. I was one of them, yet I was with the Americans. Many of them asked questions of me and I answered them. They asked, "Are the Americans serious?" They asked, "Do you think Bush will do something?" "Yes, yes," I said, "as long as you do what you are doing now." I shook hands, talked about their lives and mine and communicated silently with strangers and knew that these people sensed the weight of the moment. They did their part; they stood peacefully and silently in lines, and, by their vote, they gave the message to the world about the dignity of a people voting under occupation to seek freedom from occupation. By their vote, Palestinians gave the most eloquent response to those who would paint them all with the broad brush of terror and fanaticism.

The Election Committee prepared for these elections for two and a half years coping with life under occupation, under conditions of siege, with check points, restrictions of mobility and of communications. Teachers, both men and women, volunteered to work at the election stations that were headed by school principals. The committee, and the people, performed admirably. Dead people did not vote, no one voted twice, and there were no chads. People stood in line in quiet dignity and in numbers. No harsh words were exchanged between candidates or their supporters and there were no serious accusations of fraud. Palestinian democracy was off to a solid start.

There were some problems. The Israelis and Palestinians negotiated a deal for the Palestinians of Jerusalem to vote in 1996. Only a small fraction was allowed to vote in the city while the majority had to vote in the West Bank. Those who voted in Jerusalem had to do so at the post offices by posting their vote in mailboxes so their residency status will remain unresolved. The same rules of 1996 applied during this election. Fewer than six thousand people were allowed to vote in the city and around one hundred and twenty thousand had to vote in the West Bank. Many Jerusalemites were unable to vote in their neighborhoods because their names were not on the list. We heard many stories about individuals who moved to several stations before they eventually went to the West Bank where they could vote. Some gave up. By noon time it was clear to the international observers and the election committee that many people who wanted to vote had difficulties, so the stations were held open for all qualified voters and the hours were extended until 9 p.m. rather than 7 p.m. Some staff members of the election committee objected to the change of rules to extend voting time to 9 p.m. Several members resigned later on over their concern for the integrity of future parliamentary elections but they clearly mentioned that they believed that the changes they objected to had no impact on the outcome of current elections. None of the nine commissioners of the Committee resigned. The over 800 international monitors certified the elections without reservations as free and fair. We heard of no evidence of Israel interfering with or impeding access to elections.

The people have spoken and with just under 70% having voted, Mr. Abbas was elected by over 62%, and the runner up received 19%. Mr. Abbas's base of support far exceeded his own party—Fatah's-base of about 30%. The silent majority voted for Abbas' message of peaceful negotiations.

The Palestinian people have created their democracy. Now, they must have their freedom. The 3.5 million Palestinians in the occupied territories are not citizens of the state that rules them, or any other state. What can the meaning of liberty and self-government be without the fundamental prerequisite of citizenship? They are the largest stateless group in a world composed of citizens of nation-states. Moreover, they have been suffering under more than 37 years of military occupation by Israel, which has now become the longest continuing military occupation in recent history. There is no people on earth more badly in need of freedom than the Palestinians.

On January 9, Mr. Abbas gained legitimacy. What he now needs is to enhance and to use power and authority. One major asset that he has established is his own credibility. During his one hundred days as prime minister under Arafat, during his "wilderness" days out of office and out of favor, during his election campaign, and consistently after his victory, he kept repeating his mantra of opposition to violence, his call for unifying security agencies and his pursuit of peaceful negotiations. There was no double talk and no ambiguity. I met him during all these stages and he always said the same things in private that he said in public.

It has been widely and correctly observed that the election and the victory of President Abbas have created new opportunities to resolve this most damaging of conflicts. This, together with the renewed commitment of President Bush to the Roadmap and to the creation of a Palestinian state living in peace alongside Israel, and Prime Minister Sharon's Disengagement Plan for Gaza and several settlements in the West Bank, constitute the elements for significant progress.

Mr. Abbas is in the unenviable position of presiding as a president without a state, just as the Palestinian Authority has been held to the responsibilities of a state without having the authority, sovereignty, or prerogatives of an independent state. He has courageously staked his political future, and perhaps even personal safety, on achieving freedom for his people through peaceful negotiations. The political, historical, cultural, religious, national, regional, and international forces at play in the Palestinian body politic preclude any neat and clear resolution of the question of authority and power by a democratic election. The newly elected president has to reason with adversaries, to threaten at this time only by persuasion, to explain to his opponents that alternatives are less attractive than what he has to offer. He has to come up with the arguments for giving up the use of force even if Israel persists in assassinations and in violent incursions. He has to explain why and how he could trust this American Administration with its record of unabashed support of the heavy hand of Mr. Sharon. He has to explain his views about the unconscionable cost the Palestinian people had to pay for using violence. He has to explain his strategy to his political opponents knowing full well that they are as convinced of the utility of violence as he is of its futility. As he explains, argues, and cajoles, he has to acquire a bigger stick, and perhaps he will be forced to use it.

To succeed, he needs serious assistance from all parties. He is physically and materially dependent on others—the weakened Palestinian bureaucracy, the United States, and Israel—to help him carry out most of his program. He understands that the immediate task for Palestinians is to restructure and reform the Palestinian Authority and its institutions. Having correctly identified security as the indispensable item to deliver for his people and to these two countries, he is in a position to deliver on his campaign promise. Delivering on security is worth the overwhelming risk he is undertaking, because without it there is no strategy other than a continuation of the present miserable state of affairs. There can be no compromise on a disciplined and accountable security apparatus. Without security, there is no hope for peace. That said, it is imperative to recognize that security concerns for both Palestinians and Israelis are only a first step in a process that must lead to a full peace agreement, and to understand that in the long run security can only be truly guaranteed by implementing a viable and equitable political relationship between the parties.

For the new Palestinian leadership to succeed, it is equally important to establish the rule of law and to remove the appearance and reality of corruption. Mr. Abbas' mandate may be tested in upcoming municipal and legislative elections, where opposition groups may exploit long-standing concerns about corruption and lack of social services. It is imperative that the Palestinian government have the resources needed to deliver services to its people, or others will step into the void. However, the practical difficulties for President Abbas in dealing with the problem of corruption were outlined by the leading Palestinian pollster and analyst Khalil Shikaki at a February 2, 2005, briefing at the Palestine Center in Washington DC. According to a summary of that briefing provided by the Center:

> Shikaki said that Abbas must begin the difficult task of simultaneously confronting corruption and violence. "There is no way he can do that because to fight corruption, he must deal with those persons and groups who can deliver security," acknowledged Shikaki. However, if Abbas confronts those who are able to deliver security because of his simultaneous need to deal with corruption, "there will be a big question mark about his ability to maintain the cease fire," said Shikaki. He reiterated that if Abbas does not deal with corruption, Hamas will win at least 70 to 90 percent of the local councils and that will have a determinative effect on the outcome of parliamentary elections as well as any legislative action on the issue of corruption. If Abbas decides to go after corruption, Shikaki said that he will need to confront the Fatah Central Committee, the body that nominated Abbas for the presidency, "which is going to fight him tooth and nail." He noted that Abbas has indicated that he has no intention of confronting the senior officials in the security establishment on the issue of corruption, and is instead relying completely on them to deliver security.[1]

---

[1] www.thejerusalemfund.org/images/fortherecord.php?ID=226.

The way to help President Abbas square this circle is to provide the needed financial and technical aid, and the appointment of Lt. General William Ward as "security coordinator" to supervise reform of the Palestinian security forces is a good start. Certainly, more aid and technical support will be needed in the future.

The Israeli government is clearly in a position to do much to either help or harm the credibility of the new Palestinian leadership. From Israel, President Abbas needs cooperation and coordination. Israel has a variety of carrots and sticks and it can help lay the foundation of peace if it uses them to restructure the Palestinian-Israeli relation to one of potential partners bound together by the shared destiny of eternal neighbors. What matters is the strategic realignment that the moment promises. Forces of accommodation and reconciliation on both sides can empower each other now, leaving the logic of the zero-sum game behind. Forward-looking new thinking, away from tribal, nationalistic, and religious hostile instincts is urgently called for. What is needed now is to coordinate moves that provide the mechanisms for separation of potential partners as they work out the framework of a historic compromise.

The 37-year long occupation has been extremely onerous to the Palestinian people, as the following synopses illustrate on four key points: settlements and land expropriation, the separation barrier, checkpoints, and home demolitions.

Settlements and Land Expropriation

According to the Israeli human rights group B'Tselem, "Over the past 35 years, Israel has used a complex legal and bureaucratic mechanism to take control of more than fifty percent of the land in the West Bank."[2]

Israel has used this process to establish hundreds of settlements in the West Bank and to populate them with hundreds of thousands of Israeli citizens, preventing Palestinians from legally retaining ownership of or using these lands. According to B'Tselem:

> Since 1967, each Israeli government has...expand[ed] the settlements in the Occupied Territories, both in terms of the area of land they occupy and in terms of population. As a result of this policy, approximately 380,000 Israeli citizens now live on the settlements in the West Bank, including those established in East Jerusalem.[3]

The settlement infrastructure includes approximately 400 miles of bypass roads that crisscross the West Bank and Gaza.[4]

---
[2] www.btselem.org/english/Settlements/Land_Takeover.
[3] www.btselem.org/English/Settlements/Index.asp.
[4] www.btselem.org/english/statistics/20043112_2004_statistics.asp.

These roads are designated for Israeli-only use thereby forbidding Palestinians from using them. Successive American administrations going back to President Carter (including Presidents Reagan, Bush, Clinton, and the current President Bush), have opposed the policy of the government of Israel on settlements. Furthermore, the Geneva Conventions clearly prohibits an occupying power from transferring citizens from its own territory to the occupied territory. Settlement construction increased by 35% in 2003, and "between 1993 and 2000 the number of settlers on the West Bank (excluding East Jerusalem) increased by almost 100 percent" despite opposition to them.[5] A poll conducted by the pro-Israel peace organization Americans for Peace Now in July 2003, found that 8 out of 10 settlers would agree to return to Israel if compensated.

The Separation Barrier

The construction of the 455-mile long barrier in the West Bank is a major problem for the Palestinians since its current path cuts off hundreds of thousands of acres of Palestinian real estate.[6] The barrier's path would have been more appropriately built along the internationally recognized boundary between Israel and the occupied West Bank. A United Nations fact-finding mission in November 2003 discovered that only 11% of the barrier's route as planned at the time coincided with the green line. The remaining 89% curved deep into Palestinian territory (this has now been revised to 85%, as noted below). The Palestinians have challenged the legality of the route and the International Court of Justice (ICJ) in the Hague ruled that the path was illegal. Yet barrier construction inside the West Bank continues. A September 2004 report by the UN Office for Coordination of Humanitarian Affairs (OCHA) states:

> A new Barrier map was issued by the Israeli Ministry of Defense on 30 June 2004, altering prior routes published on 23 October 2003 and 25 March 2004. The revised route places fewer Palestinians on the west side of the Barrier but does not reduce significantly the amount of land from which the Barrier separates Palestinian landowners and farmers from their land. The revised route removes two large enclaves in the Salfit and Ramallah governorates from the prior route. However, two major roads generally prohibited for Palestinian use run across the open side of the revised route, and effectively act as barriers to Palestinian movement out of these areas. Accordingly, it is unlikely that this revision will improve the humanitarian access for the majority of Palestinians. The revised route creates two semi-enclaves and an additional four new enclaves. The revised route reduces the total length of the Barrier by 16 kilometers.

---
[5]www.btselem.org/English/Settlements/Index.asp.
[6]"Middle East Peace." *CQ Researcher*. January 2005.

The report also noted that "While part of the Barrier runs along the 1949 Armistice or the Green Line, approximately 85% of the revised planned route of the Barrier intrudes into the West Bank, up to 22 kilometers in the case of the Ari'el 'finger.'"[7]

Checkpoints

The Israeli system of checkpoints and roadblocks in the occupied territories severely inhibit the Palestinian people from carrying out an ordinary life. According to the "Country Reports on Human Rights Practices-2003, Israel and the Occupied Territories" published by the US State Department:[8]

- "Each day, tens of thousands of Palestinians traveling between Palestinian towns and villages faced as many as 730 different barriers to movement."
- "Israeli security forces harassed and abused Palestinian pedestrians and drivers who attempted to pass through the approximately 430 Israeli-controlled checkpoints in the occupied territories."
- "The Israeli Government severely restricted freedom of movement for Palestinians [by enforcing] a massive network of checkpoints and roadblocks across the occupied territories, which impeded the movement of people and goods between Palestinian cities, villages, and towns."
- "Economic problems and checkpoint obstacles affected the availability of food to Palestinian children. During the year, USAID and Johns Hopkins University reported that 7.8 percent of Palestinian children under 5 suffered from acute malnutrition, 11.7 percent suffered chronic malnutrition, and 44 percent were anemic."
- "Israeli security forces at checkpoints often impeded the provision of medical assistance to sick and injured Palestinians."

Home Demolitions

Human rights groups estimate that more than 20,000 Palestinian homes were demolished by Israeli occupation forces from 1967 to the early 1990s. Over the last four years, Israel has demolished more than 3,000 homes, leaving tens of thousands of men, women, and children homeless or without a livelihood. In a May 2004 report, Amnesty International said "Israel's unjustified destruction of thousands of Palestinian and Arab Israeli homes as well as vast areas of agricultural land has reached an unprecedented level and must stop immediately." Amnesty continued, "In the Occupied Territories, demolitions are often carried

---

[7] www.humanitarianinfo.org/opt/docs/UN/OCHA/BARRIER-REP_Update-4_%5BEn%5D-Sep2004.pdf.
[8] www.state.gov/g/drl/rls/hrrpt/2003/27929.htm.

out as collective punishments for Palestinian attacks or to facilitate the expansion of illegal Israeli settlements. Both practices contravene international law and some of these acts are war crimes."[9]

In addition, it should be noted that in the past 4 years of violence, more than 1,000 Israelis and 3,500 Palestinians have been killed, most of them on both sides unarmed civilians. The security of one people cannot be separated from security of the other—both must be protected. Honorable, competent leaders are the key to lead both people at this most difficult period of transition at a time where trust is the most precious commodity. We all know what is needed on the Israeli side to achieve this; fewer checkpoints, end of humiliation, relief from violence by settlers and the Israeli military, release of prisoners, and military withdrawal. Last but certainly not least is creating no new "realities on the ground" that contradict the vision laid out by President Bush or the Roadmap, such as settlement or outpost growth, home demolitions, land confiscation, and predetermining final status issues such as borders and Jerusalem through the route of the West Bank barrier. Helping Mr. Abbas to deliver results for his people must be as much a litmus test of Mr. Sharon's credibility as Mr. Abbas's moves on security are properly a test of his.

As for the US, President Bush has set exactly the right tone since his reelection by reiterating his commitment to the Roadmap and to his vision of a two-state peace that he outlined in his speech of June 24, 2002. He has said a Palestinian state can be born before the end of his second term. President Bush understands that the high expectations of this moment need to be reflected in a palpable improvement in the daily lives of the Palestinian people, and he is sending the right message. He has sent Secretary Rice to visit Israel and the Palestinian Territories in her first trip abroad, designated Lt. Gen. William Ward "security coordinator" for the region, and has asked the Congress for $150 million in FY06 economic assistance and an expected $200 million in the upcoming supplemental request. Our President is asking you to lend him your bi-partisan support, for this tangible and timely assistance, which sets an example for the rest of world to emulate.

President Abbas urgently needs our good offices and assistance, ranging from financial to educational, civic, cultural, technical, trade, and security issues. He has no state and his country is under occupation. He has a budget deficit of 650 million dollars for this fiscal year and has 120,000 employees on his payroll. Many of them serve in a fragmented security apparatus and a bloated bureaucracy. Many need to be sent home in order to build an efficient functional state apparatus. Learning from the Iraq model, it is wise to send them on a pension. This alone will cost hundreds of millions of dollars. He needs to rebuild the foundations of all aspects of his nation top to bottom. Without effective external help he is guaranteed to fail.

---

[9] "Under the Rubble: House Demolition and Destruction of Land and Property," Amnesty International, Report, May 18, 2004, web.amnesty.org/library/index/engmdel50332004.

We have within our grasp not just the opportunity to lay the foundation for an end to conflict, but also to foster a strategic realignment where Palestine will be an ally of the US and a partner to Israel in peace. Ultimately, security and peace will be achieved by establishing a viable, contiguous, independent, and democratic Palestinian state, with a shared Jerusalem serving as a capital for two states, and with a fair solution to the refugee problem according to international law. The "painful concession" Israel must make is to return the occupied Palestinian territories to their rightful owners. However, for this year of 2005, three tasks must be accomplished:

1. Establishing close security cooperation, with active US support. Prompt activation of committees established in Sharm al-Sheikh with scrupulous implementation of agreements by both parties.
2. Both parties implementing their commitments under the Roadmap, as they coordinate the Disengagement Plan.
3. Reforming and restructuring the Palestinian Authority.

With active US engagement, these tasks can be accomplished. In order to achieve significant progress, Palestinians need to create order and security, and Israel must refrain from implementing any unilateral measures that can prejudge the outcome of final status issues such as borders, refugees, settlements, and the status of Jerusalem. Both parties must abide by the conditions of the Roadmap.

1. Establishing close security cooperation between Israel and the Palestinian Authority, with active US support. Prompt activation of committees established in Sharm al-Sheikh with scrupulous implementation of agreements by both parties

The successful deployment of Palestinian police in northern and southern Gaza is a manifestation of early security cooperation between Israelis and Palestinians. With the declaration of the ceasefire at the Sharm al-Sheikh summit, such cooperation will only intensify as Israel prepares to redeploy from five Palestinian cities in the coming weeks, to be followed by a more comprehensive redeployment and the Gaza Disengagement Plan. Each instance of cooperation will serve to build trust between both sides and establish momentum for future cooperation. The appointment by President Bush of Lt. General William Ward as "security coordinator" to supervise reform of the Palestinian security forces is a positive first step by the US and an example of the hands-on and active approach required as Israelis and Palestinians take these first tentative measures towards rebuilding trust and confidence.

At the conclusion of the Sharm al-Sheikh summit, five committees were appointed to follow up on outstanding issues. These committees must be activated promptly and their decisions must be implemented scrupulously. No confidence building measures are better than verifying implementation of agreements and the US will be playing a crucial role in this process.

2. Both parties implementing their commitments under the Roadmap, as they coordinate the Disengagement Plan from Gaza and parts of the West Bank

Israel's Disengagement Plan from Gaza and parts of the West Bank has been welcomed by all parties as complementary to the Roadmap, and, although initially a unilateral Israeli action, it is now likely to be a coordinated effort. A joint security committee has already been established, and is scheduled to start meetings to ensure an orderly, secure, and successful Israeli withdrawal.

While most Palestinians are suspicious of Israeli Prime Minister Sharon's intentions, his plan means the irreversible end to a Greater Israel based on metaphysical and religious claims. Nonetheless, it is incumbent upon both parties to live up to their responsibilities to ensure that the disengagement is successful and serves as momentum for further moves towards peace. It is essential that Palestinian leaders and police ensure that the Israeli disengagement is not conducted 'under fire' and can serve as a precursor and model for future Israeli withdrawals. Israeli responsibilities, however, include undertaking a real end to the occupation of Gaza and a more comprehensive approach to the Disengagement Plan. Such an approach will serve to place the disengagement in the political context of a final and comprehensive agreement in order to alleviate deeply held Palestinian concerns that the Disengagement Plan is an attempt to buy time to consolidate Israel's hold on the West Bank.

Phase One of the Roadmap shoulders the Palestinians with the responsibilities of ending terror and violence, and building Palestinian institutions. Since the passing of President Yasser Arafat, the new leadership has made significant strides in meeting these responsibilities. The Palestinian elections held on January 9, 2005, under occupation, heralded the birth of Palestinian democracy, placing the Palestinians at the forefront of Arab democratization efforts. While there still remain provisions under Phase One of the Roadmap for the Palestinians to implement, in the four weeks since the elections (that were themselves a Roadmap provision), the Palestinian leadership has reiterated its commitment to implementing its Roadmap responsibilities, has successfully negotiated a ceasefire pledge from Palestinian militant groups, has instructed official Palestinian media to abstain from any statements or messages that may be construed as incitement, and has deployed thousands of Palestinian police in the Gaza Strip.

Israel's primary responsibility under Phase One, an end to settlement activities including "natural growth" of existing settlements, has yet to be fulfilled in any meaningful sense. On February 7, 2005, the *Washington Post* reported that:

> The Israeli government and private Jewish groups are working in concert to build a human cordon around Jerusalem's Old City and its disputed holy sites, moving Jewish residents into Arab neighborhoods to consolidate their grip on strategic locations, according to critics of the effort and a Washington Post investigation. The goal is to establish Jewish enclaves in and around Arab-dominated East Jerusalem and eventually link them to form a ring around the city, a key battleground in the decades-long Israeli-Palestinian conflict because of its Jewish and Muslim holy sites, according to activists involve in the effort and critics of the campaign.[10]

Such aggressive settlement activity is a clear example of how unilateral measures designed to prejudice critical final status issues serve as an obstacle to realizing President Bush's vision of peace based on two states, and why ending such activities is the primary Israeli responsibility under Phase One of the Roadmap.

3. Reform and Restructuring of the Palestinian Authority

Establishing the rule of law is the main and immediate task facing the new presidency of Mr. Abbas. More specifically, the two main areas of reform that are essential for the Palestinians to address are those of corruption and restructuring and unifying the security services. It is important to stress that these areas of reform can and should proceed independently of the Israeli-Palestinian peace track. They are reforms essential to the Palestinian national interest and serve in laying the groundwork for building the representative and accountable institutions necessary for a robust democracy. The participation of Secretary of State Rice in the upcoming March 1-2 conference in London, which will focus on building institutions that will form the bedrock of a Palestinian state, is an important and timely contribution. We urge Congress to support the President and the Administration by authorizing the necessary funds to assist in building these vital institutions.

The Palestinians have made impressive strides in addressing corruption and managing Palestinian finances to be transparent and attractive to international donors. While work on this ongoing process remains to be done, Finance Minister Salam Fayyad, recognized worldwide for his

---

[10]"Israelis Act to Encircle East Jerusalem," *Washington Post*, February 7, 2005; A15.

credibility and reputability, has made great strides and demonstrated serious diligence in working to accomplish this priority. As an example, the Palestinian national budget is the only one from any Arab country to be posted online.

Security is the indispensable item for Mr. Abbas to deliver, both for his people and for Israelis. Delivering on security is worth the overwhelming risk he is undertaking because without security there is no peace strategy. The ceasefire declaring a formal end to more than four years of fighting by both parties at the summit held in Egypt on Tuesday, February 8, 2005, is an early and positive sign of Mr. Abbas' appreciation and seriousness about this issue. The appointing of a new Palestinian security chief to oversee the process of unifying and training the Palestinian security services is another critical component of restructuring the Palestinian Authority.

Conclusion

The unique promise of this moment is the commitment of the current political leadership on all three sides to perform these tasks, combined with the will of the majority of Palestinians, Israelis, and Americans for peace. For this promise to lead to peace, the indispensable leadership of the US needs to come in the form of such tangible, hands-on mechanisms. We can encourage world leaders to lend a hand in securing peace. We can set up the system of ultimate security for both parties by incorporating them in a binding international alliance. Once we are able to deliver help to the people on the ground, we should make sure to be public and clear about our support for Mr. Abbas and the Palestinian people.

While resolving the Israeli-Palestinian conflict is properly the main focus of our present attention and efforts, the ultimate goal must be the creation of a comprehensive regional peace in the Middle East. The constructive involvement of Egypt and Jordan is a significant indicator for prospects of such a comprehensive peace. The fact that these two countries participated in the summit at Sharm al-Sheikh earlier this week points to the broad constituency within the region for a Palestinian-Israeli peace.

To be sure, there are those in Palestine, Israel, the Arab world, and here in the US who are opposed to the peaceful vision of a two-state solution. We will hear their belligerent words and we should anticipate their nefarious deeds. Our challenge is to build successes and tangible benefits that promote a culture of reconciliation and peace, and defeat the forces of hate and violence. Peace in Palestine will deny demagogues and terrorists the most potent weapon in their arsenal.

The urgency of timely intervention cannot be overstated, as what all parties do and do not do in the coming months will determine whether this glimmer of hope becomes the dawn of a new era of peace, or proves to be merely the twilight before another long night of conflict and chaos. We must act decisively in the interests of the Israeli, Palestinian, and Arab peoples, and, above all, in our own American national interest.

The summit at Sharm al-Sheikh, the initial points of agreement between the parties and the prompt initial steps taken to implement them, are the most promising developments in many years. We cannot afford to fail to seize this opportunity and commit substantial efforts and resources to achieve peace.

POSTSCRIPT

ATFP urges all those who agree with the tenets, strategies, and propositions contained in this short collection to join with us in advancing the only viable solution for ending this most long-lasting and damaging of conflicts. ATFP welcomes the support and participation of all people who share these views. In particular, we urge Palestinian-Americans to join us in emphasizing both their role as patriotic American citizens and the importance of Palestinian independence for the American national interest. We also appeal to all other Americans, especially Jewish Americans who understand the virtue of our approach to the issue, to join us in dialogue and partnership to advance what ought to be a mutual agenda. We must form a broad-based alliance in which disparate groups and individuals, with their own diverse reasons and interests, may join together to secure freedom for the Palestinians, peace for Israel and all states in the Middle East, and enhanced national security for our country, the United States.

The editors wish to thank the Board of Directors of ATFP, its President, Dr. Ziad Asali, and Executive Director, Rafi Dajani, for making both the work of the organization and the production of this short book possible.

AMERICAN TASK FORCE ON PALESTINE'S EXECUTIVE STAFF AND BOARD OF DIRECTORS

Executive Staff

Ziad Asali, MD, President
Rafi Dajani, Executive Director
Hussein Ibish, Ph.D., Senior Fellow

Board of Directors

Ziad Asali, MD
Naila Asali
Amjad Atallah, Esq.
Abed Awad, Esq.
Jesse I. Aweida
Peter Aweida
Tawfiq Barqawi
Nedal Deeb, Ph.D.
Ameen Estaiteyeh
George Hishmeh
Maha Kaddoura
Omar M. Kader, Ph.D.
Bishop Samir Kafity
Shadia Kanaan
Rashid Khatib
Hani Masri
Farah Munayyer
Joey Musmar
Ferial Polhill
Fahim Qubain
Joseph Qutub
Rana Sadik
Tareq Salahi
George Salem, Esq.
Saliba Sarsar, Ph.D.
Zuhair Suidan
Cheryl Sukhtian
Basel Yanes, M.D.

THE EDITORS

Hussein Ibish is Senior Fellow at the American Task Force on Palestine (ATFP) and Executive Director of the Hala Salaam Maksoud Foundation for Arab-American Leadership. From 1998-2004, he served as Communications Director for the American-Arab Anti-Discrimination Committee (ADC), the largest Arab-American membership organization in the US. He has made numerous radio and television appearances, and has written for many newspapers, including the *Los Angeles Times*, the *Washington Post* and the *Chicago Tribune*, and was Washington Correspondent for the *Daily Star* (Beirut). Ibish is editor and principle author of 2 major studies of *Hate Crimes and Discrimination against Arab Americans 1998-2000* (ADC, 2001) and *Sept. 11, 2001-Oct. 11, 2002* (ADC, 2003). He is author of "At the Constitution's Edge: Arab Americans and Civil Liberties in the US" in *States of Confinement* (St. Martin's Press, 2000), "Anti-Arab Bias in American Policy and Discourse" in *Race in 21st Century America* (Michigan State University Press, 2001), "Race and the War on Terror," in *Race and Human Rights* (Michigan State University Press, 2005) and "Symptoms of Alienation: How Arab and American Media View Each Other" in *Arab Media in the Information Age* (ECSSR, 2005). He is also the author, along with Ali Abunimah, of "The Palestinian Right of Return" (ADC, 2001) and "The Media and the New Intifada" in *The New Intifada* (Verso, 2001). From 2001-2004 Ibish was Vice-President of the National Coalition to Protect Political Freedom. He has a Ph.D. in Comparative Literature from the University of Massachusetts, Amherst.

Saliba Sarsar is Associate Vice President for Academic Program Initiatives and Professor of Political Science at Monmouth University. He received a B.A. in political science and history interdisciplinary, *summa cum laude*, from Monmouth College in 1978 and his Ph.D. from Rutgers University in political science in 1984. His articles have appeared in *Peace and Conflict Studies, Holy Land Studies, Palestine-Israel Journal of Politics, Economics and Culture*; *Peace Review: A Journal of Social Justice*; *Middle East Quarterly*; *Jerusalem Quarterly File*; and *Journal of South Asian and Middle East Studies*, among others. He guest edited a special issue of the *International Journal of Politics, Culture, and Society*, focusing on Palestinian-Israeli relations. He is co-author of *Ideology, Values, and Technology in Political Life* and *World Politics: An Interdisciplinary Approach*. He is also editor of *Education for Leadership and Social Responsibility*. Sarsar has been interviewed by NJN (*Inside Trenton* and *NJ Caucus*); Comcast (*Meet the Leaders*); CN8; WMBC-TV; Voice of America (*Point of View*); WJLK; WMCX; Wisconsin Public Radio; Radio Jamaica (*Beyond the Headlines*); CFRB 1010 AM, Canada ("Toronto at Noon"); *New York Times*; *Seattle Times*; and *Asbury Park Press (APP)*. His editorials have appeared in *APP, USA Today*, and *New Jersey Jewish News*, and the *National Herald*. In recognition for his dialogue activities between Arab Americans and

Jewish Americans, he received the *Humanitarian Award* from the National Conference for Community and Justice in September 2001. In April 2003, Sarsar was featured in *The New York Times*, "His Mission: Finding Why People Fight—A Witness to Mideast Conflict Turns to Dialogue and Peace." Section 14, New Jersey, pages 1, 4. Sarsar, born in Jerusalem, is an American citizen. He is married to Hiyam Zakharia, also from Jerusalem, and they have two young daughters, NoorEvelyn and Hania.